PLAYING WITH FIRE

PHOENIX RIDGE FIRE DEPT
BOOK 8

EMILY HAYES

1

CASS

Thick, acrid smoke billowed from the shattered windows of the old brick building, curling into the night sky like dark, twisting tendrils that blotted out the stars. Inside, the fire roared with a fierce, unrelenting intensity, casting an eerie orange glow that pulsed through the thick smoke, illuminating the shifting shadows within. Flames licked hungrily at the wooden beams of the ceiling, which groaned under the heat, sending sparks and embers spiraling into the air.

The restaurant's interior had become a furnace of chaos. Tables and chairs were overturned, their shapes warped and twisted, caught in the hungry jaws of the inferno. In the kitchen, the clatter of metal pans falling from their racks added a chilling soundtrack to the disaster. Every few seconds, the fire grew louder, its roar punctuated by the sharp, piercing pops of glass jars shattering, their contents spilling and fueling the flames. The old electrical wiring sparked and crackled along the walls, sending a shower of sizzling embers across the floor.

Captain Cassidy Harris stood just beyond the engulfed entrance, barking commands with a voice that cut through the noise. Her helmet was pulled low over her eyes, shielding her gaze from the flames as she directed her team with calm authority. Her face was streaked with soot and sweat, rivulets running down her cheeks, tracing patterns through the grime. Every muscle was taut, her senses sharp as she watched the inferno with the practiced focus of someone who knew just how unpredictable fire could be.

"Engine 3, cover the rear left! The fire's spreading toward the restaurant's kitchen." Her voice was steady, even as the heat washed over her, fierce and unforgiving.

Fires like this one were nothing new to her, after all.

She saw her lieutenant, Sara Perez, nod before relaying her command down the line without hesitation.

It had not been long since the legendary Fire Chief Becky Thompson had retired, flitting off to travel the world. (Whether it was a permanent retirement or not, who knew with Becky) And while Cass knew her team trusted her, Becky's boots were intimidating to fill in her promotion to Acting Chief.

Shaking her head, Cass brought herself back to the here and now. She couldn't allow herself to be distracted from the task at hand —especially not after the email that had landed in her inbox at the start of her shift. The city was sending out a consultant. They wouldn't have dared try it under Becky Thompson's reign, but now she was out of the way, all the pencil pushers had started jostling over who would revitalize all the public sectors. Not that much revitalization ever happened. No. It was always cuts, cuts, and more cuts.

Evelyn Ford was the name of the consultant, apparently. She'd be visiting the department in a day or so, no doubt scribbling notes on a clipboard and sneering at the vital work her team did—while never putting in a hard day's work in her life, Cass would bet. She'd looked her up, of course. Evelyn had cut her way through a slew of government sectors in the last few years, and before that, she'd had a cushy job in finance. How someone like that was supposed to know what was best for life-saving services, Cass would never know.

Donelli's Pizza. The lettering above the door had been all but singed away, the edges of the plastic name melted and curling. The place had been a staple of Phoenix Ridge for decades. Cass only hoped the insurance would be enough to rebuild. She herself had spent countless meals there as a child, and even now it was her go-to spot when she was craving something quick and greasy. It'd be a shame to see it go for good.

Cass scanned the scene before her, eyes narrowing as she picked out each member of her crew amid the chaotic haze and flashing lights. Every move they made filled her with pride. These were *her* people, her family in all but blood. The legacy that Chief

Thompson had left behind for her to continue.

"Captain, we've got everyone out of the restaurant and the neighboring buildings. All civilians are gathered out on the east side." Sara's voice crackled down her radio.

Relief came in a quick and fleeting breath. Cass nodded to herself, her eyes darting up to the second story where flames were licking hungrily at the window frames, eager to claim even more of the building.

"Good job. Ladders at the ready. On my mark—get the water up there and reinforce the eastern side. We're cutting off the supports below. Now," she ordered, moving with practiced ease, her boots crunching on the ash-dusted asphalt. The last thing she needed was for the ceiling to collapse and feed the fire further. They were already at risk of it ballooning if it made it through the gas connection.

The firefighters moved in unison, each trained motion honed through countless drills and real-life rescues. They spread out, a seamless line of professionals, their reflective gear catching flickers of light from the blazing restaurant. One team wrestled a heavy-duty hose into position, its nozzle aimed directly at the towering flames licking out of the windows. With a nod from Cass, they unleashed a powerful stream of water, the mist hissing and steaming as it hit the intense heat.

On Cass's cue, the ladder team sprang into action. Two firefighters, grunting with the strain, extended a massive metal ladder to the eastern side of the building, anchoring it into place with a sharp clang. Within seconds, a firefighter was climbing up, hauling an extra hose and equipment as she moved. Her partner followed close behind, ready to reinforce her and work in tandem to get the water into the heart of the blaze.

Nearby, another group hacked away at a section of the building's support with heavy axes, moving quickly but cautiously to create a break in the structure's beams below. They worked in pairs—one steadying while the other struck with precision, metal biting into wood with a rhythmic thunk. Each blow was timed to avoid further stress on the building, reducing the risk of the ceiling caving in and spreading the flames into new areas.

Meanwhile, a small crew worked diligently near the gas line, carefully inspecting the pipes for signs of danger. Sweat glistened on their brows despite the chill of the night air, their movements deliberate, knowing that any small rupture could transform the fire into an uncontrollable explosion.

As Cass moved from team to team, her words of encouragement and sharp instructions kept everyone focused. Her presence seemed to anchor them, her voice cutting through the roar of the flames.

For just a moment, the roar of the fire dulled, and Cass focused on the steady rhythm of her heartbeat, fast but controlled. Unbidden, Becky's last words before leaving came to her, echoing the advice she'd given Cass over and over through the years. "*Trust your gut, Cass. It won't lead you astray.*"

The level of trust Becky had in her usually unnerved her, but tonight it only strengthened her. A rush of determination flared in her chest, merging seamlessly with her next shouted command.

Her team worked like a single, fluid organism, their steps a well-rehearsed routine, guided by her commands. Time stood still, minutes and seconds stretched as they fought against their ferocious and primal adversary. There was danger in their line of work—they all knew that day after day as they risked their lives—but there was beauty in it too. Beauty as they saved others from peril; beauty as they watched the final flames ebb into embers.

The fire's resistance wavered as it struggled for life, then finally, with a last sullen spit of sparks, it relinquished its hold, sputtering out. Cass stood amidst the swirling remnants of smoke and wafts of plastic fumes, breathing hard as adrenaline pulsed a diminishing beat through her veins. She glanced around at her team, their faces streaked with exhaustion but proud, triumphant smiles tugging at their lips.

"Great work, everyone," she called, her voice carrying over the clatter of their equipment and sirens. As the last glowing embers were doused and police moved in to secure the area, Cass felt the weight of everyone's expectations settle comfortably across her shoulders. Becky was not here and they had been fine. They'd held the line tonight, and damn if she wasn't proud of that.

Still, the night was yet young. Their debrief awaited them, and with it, the specter of whatever this new city consultant would bring with her.

The sharp scent of smoke still lingered in Cass's hair as she pushed open the heavy door to the briefing room. The fluorescent lights overhead cast a stark glow onto the scuffed table in the center of the room, illuminating the worn, sweat-streaked faces of her crew as they slumped into the weathered chairs that surrounded the table. The post-operations debriefing was a familiar ritual to them all, a time to talk through the battle they'd just fought, analyze their performance, work through any problems, and rally themselves for the next inevitable call.

Cass's gaze swept over the room, taking in the nods and tired smiles directed her way. The team settled themselves into their chairs, their energy spent, their uniforms still smudged with ash. Just as she opened her mouth to begin, the click of heels sounded in the hallway. Measured and deliberate. The atmosphere in the room shifted, the firefighters sitting up straighter and adjusting their uniforms, all the while darting glances toward the doorway.

Tall and impeccably dressed in a tailored blazer and pencil skirt, Evelyn Ford stepped into the room, a sharp silhouette against the scuffed walls. Clutched between her perfectly manicured hands, she held a tablet, which she finished tapping away on as she crossed the threshold into the briefing room. Her sharp gray eyes scanned the room with a critical detachment that made Cass's lungs tighten. Silence pooled in her wake, broken only by the creak of chairs as everyone turned to look at her.

"Captain Harris?" she said, her tone low and modulated; every syllable was as crisp and precise as her appearance.

Cass pushed down the pulse that quickened unexpectedly at the sound and forced her muscles to relax; an attempt at a smile spread across her mouth. She stepped forward and extended a hand, firm and direct. The touch was brief, and Evelyn's smooth palm was a striking contrast to her own hardened, calloused one.

"Ms. Ford, I'm surprised you decided to

pay us a visit so late in the day. Or so early, I should say." Cass glanced at the clock on the wall that read 1:35 a.m. God, it was late; only a few hours left to go before the end of their shift. "We were just about to begin the debrief."

Evelyn nodded, the barest tilt of her head. "I'll stay out of your way for now, Captain. Don't mind me; I'll just observe from the corner. You have my admiration for your actions tonight. You and your team were most...effective."

Cass caught the slight pause before the word, as though Evelyn were sifting through her mental lexicon for the most clinically accurate compliment available. A murmur of approval ran through the team, but Cass's jaw tightened at the faint edge to the consultant's tone. She took her seat at the head of the table, eyes never straying far from Evelyn. She knew there was only ever one reason the city would send in a consultant. Cuts. She wouldn't give Evelyn Ford any opportunity to get rid of a single member of her team. Her family. Becky had entrusted them into her care, and she sure as hell wasn't going to betray that trust.

The consultant moved a few steps closer, her tablet balanced in one hand. "That said, I'll be introducing some procedural enhancements in the coming weeks—strategies to align with the city's new operational efficiency standards."

There it was. The room seemed to grow colder, a chill of apprehension threading through Cass's spine. Her fingers curled against the table, knuckles whitening. She forced herself to exhale and keep her voice even. "I'm sure we can discuss those changes in detail when the time comes. But this team's strength lies in its cohesion, its trust. That's something we're not willing to compromise."

The flicker of acknowledgment in Evelyn's eyes was so brief Cass almost thought she'd imagined it. "Of course," Evelyn said, her tone polite but unyielding. "Efficiency need not come at the cost of camaraderie, Captain. In fact, it's essential to foster both."

The conversation lapsed, Evelyn's gaze sweeping the room once more before settling on Cass. A ghost of a smile threatened at the corner of Cass's mouth, quickly subdued as she read the unspoken challenge there.

As Evelyn turned, tapping a few notes on her tablet before leaving, Cass found herself watching the sway of her stride with an inexplicable tightness in her chest. A storm was coming.

Cass stood in the doorway of the conference room, arms crossed over her chest, her jaw clenched tight as she watched Evelyn stride down the hallway. Evelyn's sharp heels echoed against the linoleum, a brisk, unrelenting rhythm that seemed to mock Cass's slower, deliberate world. Evelyn didn't belong here, not in the heart of the Phoenix Ridge Fire Station, where the air carried the faint scent of smoke and sweat and every corner told stories of camaraderie forged in the heat of danger. Yet Evelyn had walked in with her tailored suit and clipboard as if she owned the place—or worse, like she understood it. The air in the conference room shifted as Evelyn's heels clacked down the hallway, each step receding until silence reclaimed the space. A beat passed, then another before the murmurs started—a low hum of speculation and nervous energy.

"Think she's here to make us run drills

until we drop?" a young firefighter, Ortiz, muttered with a lopsided grin.

Her attempt at humor fell into the silence, met with a few chuckles that sounded more forced than genuine. Cass glanced at her, appreciating the effort, even if the tension in the room barely wavered.

"She's got that look to her, doesn't she?" Perez said, shaking her head with a mock shudder. "Corporate types always think they know what's best."

"Enough," Cass said, not unkindly. The room quieted, eyes shifting to her for guidance, reassurance. She softened her voice. "We handle this like we handle everything else. One step at a time, with our heads up. No consultant is going to shake what we've built here."

Satisfied by the murmured nods and a few smirks of agreement, Cass leaned back in her chair as the crew began to disperse. The scrape of chairs and shuffle of boots faded into the background until she was alone, the ambient hum of the station filling the void. She stood slowly, her gaze caught by a movement outside the window.

Evelyn stood by her car, bathed in the unforgiving glow of the parking lot lights. She was tapping briskly on her tablet, brows furrowed in concentration. Cass studied her from the shadowed room, trying to read more than the practiced mask of efficiency and authority. The consultant's calm, unyielding demeanor had already left its imprint in Cass's thoughts, a friction she couldn't quite shake.

Why does she have to come in and disrupt everything? The question pulsed in her mind, but it wasn't only irritation that buzzed beneath the surface. Cass pressed her fingers against the cool edge of the table, memories of the fire they'd just fought mixing with the fresh tension of Evelyn's presence. The department was more than a team—it was a family, a testament to Chief Thompson's legacy and Cass's own blood, sweat, and stubborn resolve.

Yet there was more than just wariness coiling within her. The brief, charged handshake, the way Evelyn's sharp eyes never faltered...Cass felt unsettled in a way she hadn't felt in years. A dissonance between being ready for a fight and something more confusing, something that made her chest tighten with an uninvited thrum of interest.

Cass clenched her jaw, dragging herself back from that thought. She could already see the battle lines being drawn, the changes Evelyn promised stirring ripples in a sea that Cass needed to keep calm. She'd defend her crew and her way of leading, even if it meant clashing with Evelyn's cold precision at every turn.

But as she caught one last glance of Evelyn slipping into her car, the memory of their handshake—firm, charged, and unreadable—lingered. Cass exhaled sharply, a vow forming like iron in her veins. *No matter what she plans, this is my department. And I won't let anyone, no matter how sharp their eyes or steady their voice, take that away.*

Cass couldn't decide which was more irritating: the way Evelyn had dismissed her concerns during the meeting with clinical detachment or the fact that she hadn't even pretended to care about the lives behind the numbers. It wasn't personal for Evelyn; it never was with people like her. They came from their sterile offices, eyes only on the bottom line, and made decisions that cut deep into the heart of people like Cass and her team. Cass could still hear Evelyn's calm, clipped voice from their meeting. *"We need to prioritize efficiency. Some tough decisions will have to be made."* Tough decisions? Cass's lips pressed into a hard line. Those "tough decisions" wouldn't just be numbers on a spreadsheet. They'd be firefighters' livelihoods, safety, and pride—things Evelyn Ford of all people couldn't possibly understand from her high-rise office.

Cass's gaze lingered on the back of Evelyn's head as she disappeared into her sleek car, her blonde hair swaying neatly with the wind. A pang of guilt stabbed through Cass for how quickly she'd written off Evelyn as the enemy, but she couldn't help it. Evelyn represented everything Cass hated about bureaucracy: the faceless systems, the calculated indifference, the refusal to see what really mattered. Cass had spent her entire career on the frontlines, where every decision carried immediate, tangible consequences. She'd held people's lives in her hands, felt the heat of raging flames, and borne the weight of loss alongside her crew. She doubted Evelyn had ever stepped foot into a burning building or dealt with the aftermath of a family shattered by tragedy.

And yet, despite Cass's simmering anger, there was something about Evelyn that made her feel...uneasy. It wasn't just the abrupt way she'd shut down Cass's arguments or the unnerving precision with which she'd dismantled the department's current budget. There was something in the way Evelyn carried herself—so cold, so composed—that made Cass feel like she was standing in front of an impenetrable wall. She hated it. Hated that Evelyn didn't flinch under her glare, didn't rise to the bait when Cass had pushed her harder than she should have.

Cass let out a sharp breath and turned back toward the room, catching sight of the rumpled notes she'd scribbled during their meeting. She'd known from the moment the city announced a consultant was coming that it wouldn't be good news, but she hadn't expected...*her*. Evelyn Ford, with her immaculate posture and brisk tone, had somehow made the inevitable feel even worse. Cass had dealt with budget cuts before, had fought tooth and nail to preserve what she could, but this felt different. Evelyn hadn't come to negotiate or to understand. She'd come to execute a plan already set in motion, and Cass was just an obstacle to be dealt with.

But damn it, Cass wasn't going to make it easy for her. The fire station wasn't just a workplace; it was a second home, a family. Every firefighter under her command wasn't just a name on a roster—they were her people, and she would protect them with everything she had. If Evelyn thought she could waltz in here and start tearing things apart without a fight, she was in for a rude awakening.

Still, as Cass replayed their conversation in her mind, a flicker of doubt crept in. Evelyn had been cold, yes, but she hadn't been cruel. There'd been no malice in her words, no unnecessary barbs. She was just detached. Professional. That only made it worse somehow because it meant she truly believed what she was doing was right. Cass didn't know if she could change Evelyn's mind, but she knew she had to try.

Dragging a hand through her hair, Cass made her way back to her desk, where more reports awaited her attention. The weight of the day pressed heavily on her shoulders, but she pushed it aside. There was too much at stake to let herself get bogged down by frustration—or by the nagging awareness of Evelyn Ford's voice lingering in her mind, sharp and precise like the point of a blade.

Cass settled into her chair and picked up her pen, her jaw tightening with resolve. She might not like Evelyn Ford—hell, she couldn't stand her right now—but this was her station, her crew, and her fight. And she wasn't about to back down.

2

EVELYN

The steady purr of the engine faded as Evelyn Ford switched off her car, the silence thickening in its absence. She took a moment to survey the fire station, an imposing structure that seemed to radiate a quiet, unyielding strength. Its brick walls held a history of sweat, camaraderie, and lives saved, stories that whispered from the shadows beyond the bay doors and the golden glow of the station lights spilling out onto the asphalt. She felt a chill that wasn't from the cool evening air.

Evelyn straightened, smoothing down her crisp blazer with practiced efficiency. Her reflection in the side mirror was the same one she'd seen for years: poised, confident, untouchable. She glanced at the station's crest emblazoned over the entrance and exhaled, already hearing the distant rumble of resistance she'd have to cut through. This wasn't her first time stepping into a legacy, one built on tight-knit bonds and tradition, and it wouldn't be the last.

This is just another job, she reminded herself, stepping forward with the click of her polished heels striking the pavement. But Phoenix Ridge felt different, if only because of what she'd read. Chief Becky Thompson—now a legend traveling the world—had set the gold standard for a department that prided itself not just on skill but on an unshakeable trust that bordered on family. *And families don't like outsiders,* Evelyn mused. Especially ones who came bearing changes.

Evelyn took another step, the click of her heels punctuating her thoughts as she assessed the scene before her. This wasn't her first time overhauling a department, but Phoenix Ridge presented a unique challenge. She'd come here to make things more efficient, to trim the budget in a way that would force every dollar to stretch further—a task that seemed sensible in theory but tended to feel personal to those on the receiving end.

She knew what people thought of consultants like her: outsiders who slashed budgets without understanding the heart of what they were cutting. But in her mind, this wasn't about ruthlessly stripping down; it was about strengthening from the core. Phoenix Ridge Fire Department was already excellent—Becky Thompson's legacy was proof of that—but with the city's resources stretched thin, the department needed to adapt or risk losing funding entirely. Every dollar saved could be reinvested in the long term, enabling them to update equipment, adopt cutting-edge technology, and better protect the firefighters who risked their lives.

Yet Evelyn knew she'd have to tread carefully. Change, especially in a place that prized its traditions and sense of family, would be a hard sell. She wasn't blind to the skepticism she'd felt the minute she'd walked into the firehouse—the cautious glances, the muttered words. They saw her as the enemy, an intruder threatening what they held dear. But Evelyn was here to improve things, to make the department sustainable in ways that would secure its future, even if it meant making tough decisions now.

She tried to shake off her discomfort, reminding herself that she'd done this before and that she was here to help them see beyond the immediacy of their resistance. But Phoenix Ridge felt different, as if its loyalty to its own extended beyond reason. Here, tradition wasn't just a word; it was a heartbeat, a collective pride. And she was about to put her hands on it, trying to reshape it in ways that might be necessary but would inevitably be met with distrust.

Evelyn took a steadying breath. This was her job. She was here to make things better, even if they couldn't see it yet.

Inside, the warm, smoky scent of the station enveloped her, hinting at recent use, a night spent on the job. It wasn't unpleasant, but it carried a weight that settled into her thoughts. This was the smell of the women who ran into danger without a second thought. An all female team. For a heartbeat, Evelyn allowed herself to feel a flicker of something unfamiliar, something almost like respect. She quashed it with a practiced blink.

As she walked toward the conference room, snippets of her earlier encounter with Captain Cassidy Harris played on repeat. The fire captain had been everything Evelyn anticipated—and yet not. There had been fire, not just in her commands but in her eyes, a fierce intensity that drew people in and, apparently, held them loyal beyond reason. The reports hadn't quite captured that.

Cassidy Harris's voice during the debrief had been sure, edged with defiance, a stark contrast to the crisp, calculated way Evelyn was used to working. Harris was the type who thrived in chaos, who led with her heart as much as her head. And while Evelyn knew how to deal with obstinate leaders, there was something unsettling about how Harris's presence lingered in her mind, like an ember refusing to cool.

Evelyn felt a twinge of irritation at the thought. *Resistance is part of the job,* she reminded herself, cataloging the details from their interaction. But it gnawed at her, that flicker of admiration threatening her tightly wound resolve. The captain's challenge had sparked something, an unfamiliar dissonance that Evelyn wasn't accustomed to. She quickened her pace, as if the sharp staccato of her heels could drown out the echo of Cassidy Harris's unwavering stare.

Focus, Ford, she told herself, tightening her grip on the tablet in her hand. This was no time for distractions, no matter how much heat flared from the memory of Harris's fierce eyes or the defiant tilt of her chin.

The entrance to the conference room loomed ahead. Evelyn squared her shoulders, ready to step back into the fray, where she knew loyalty would battle logic and pride would test protocol.

The hallway was a quiet corridor stretching into the heart of the fire station, lined with framed photographs that seemed to whisper stories. Evelyn's polished shoes tapped against the worn linoleum, their rhythmic click softened by the weight of the station's history pressing in around her. She glanced at the photos: firefighters, arms slung over one another's shoulders, grinning through grime and exhaustion. Images of rescues mid-action, the blur of motion and smoke captured in split seconds of triumph and relief. There were plaques, awards bearing Chief Becky Thompson's name, words like *courage* and *excellence* etched into brass.

Evelyn paused, her gaze lingering on one photo where Cassidy Harris stood front and center, her expression both fierce and protective, blue eyes alight with a determination that leapt from the frame. She felt the hint of a shiver run down her spine, a reminder of what she'd felt earlier in the night—the sense that Harris wasn't just a leader but a guardian, a force capable of pulling people into her orbit.

This is what I'm up against, Evelyn thought, fingers flexing against the tablet at her side. It wasn't just the logistics of change or the bureaucratic resistance she had anticipated. It was deeper, wound tightly around shared memories and loyalty forged under fire. She was here to streamline, to modernize, and to maximize efficiency, but that task suddenly felt heavier, more personal in this space that breathed camaraderie and trust.

As she resumed her walk, the notes from

the debriefing replayed in her mind. Harris's words had been sharp but composed, edged with a protectiveness that resonated in the room. The subtle shifts of posture among the crew, the way they looked to their captain for cues—none of it had been lost on Evelyn. It wasn't just loyalty she'd seen; it was kinship, something almost primal. The realization sparked an unease in her. Introducing changes here wouldn't be as simple as pushing policy and crunching numbers. To get any real buy-in, she'd need more than her usual strategy. She'd need to show them that she understood what they valued.

But did she? Could she? Evelyn exhaled, a barely audible sound in the quiet hallway. Winning over this department felt akin to scaling a cliff with only the thinnest rope, and right now, Cassidy Harris was the jagged peak standing defiantly in her path.

She's just a challenge, Evelyn told herself, a mantra she'd repeated many times before. Yet when she pictured Harris, the memory of their interaction tugged at the edges of her thoughts. Harris's voice, unwavering, sharp as a blade, had carried the unmistakable timbre of someone who'd fight tooth and nail for her team. The flash in her blue eyes —a mix of fire and steel—had made Evelyn's pulse quicken in a way that bothered her more than she was willing to admit.

It was infuriating. This was supposed to be a straightforward job, just another assignment to add to her list of successes. But the way Harris stood her ground, the way her presence filled a room and refused to be ignored... Evelyn shook her head, annoyed at herself for the distraction. She wanted to attribute it all to her frustration, to the defiance she'd faced, but the nagging feeling remained.

Focus, she thought, clearing her mind as she turned a corner and pushed open the door to her temporary office that contained a small desk that had been hastily cleared for her in the corner of the fire station's administrative office. She'd been given permission to use the captain's desk when the team was called out, but for now this was her home. Papers were stacked neatly before her, each one meticulously annotated with the data she needed to make her case to the city council. Outside the office window, the steady hum of activity in the station played out like a scene from a movie: firefighters bantering as they cleaned equipment, the distant blare of a radio dispatch, boots clomping on the concrete floor. It was all so...*chaotic*. And at the center of that chaos was Captain Cassidy Harris.

Evelyn leaned back in her chair, staring at the closed door of the captain's office across the room. She had barely known Harris for twenty-four hours, but already she was sure of one thing: she was going to be a problem.

The captain was everything Evelyn disliked in a professional adversary. Loud, brash, and stubborn as hell. During their meeting, Harris had made it abundantly clear that she had no intention of working *with* Evelyn. No, Harris was gearing up for a fight, and it seemed she'd decided that Evelyn was the enemy before she'd even walked through the door. That kind of hostility was exhausting—and completely unproductive.

Evelyn sighed and picked up her pen, tapping it against the edge of her notebook. Harris had come into the meeting armed with arguments and anecdotes, throwing around terms like *tradition* and *family* as though they held any weight against cold, hard numbers. Evelyn couldn't deny the fire captain's passion—it practically radiated off her—but passion didn't balance budgets or improve efficiency. It was all emotion, no strategy.

What irritated Evelyn the most, though, was the captain's unwillingness to listen. Harris had bulldozed through every point Evelyn had tried to make, interrupting her with sharp rebuttals and personal jabs. It was infuriating. Evelyn prided herself on being calm and composed, no matter the situation, but Harris had a way of pushing her buttons that felt...deliberate. Evelyn wasn't used to people like Harris—people who wore their emotions on their sleeves and charged headfirst into conflict without considering the consequences.

It wasn't that Evelyn didn't understand where Harris was coming from. She knew what the fire department meant to the captain; it was obvious in every word she spoke, in the fire that burned behind her eyes. But understanding wasn't the same as agreeing, and Evelyn couldn't let sentimentality cloud her judgment. She had a job to do, and she was going to do it, whether Cassidy Harris liked it or not.

Her gaze drifted back to the door of Harris's office. Harris had the kind of presence that drew people in, a natural charisma that made it easy to see why her crew respected her. But that same intensity could be a double-edged sword, especially when it was turned against someone like Evelyn.

If Harris thought she could intimidate Evelyn into backing down, she was in for a rude awakening. Evelyn had faced tougher opponents than the fire captain in her career, and she hadn't lost yet. Cassidy Harris might be a force to be reckoned with, but Evelyn was determined to prove that logic, reason, and a cool head would always prevail.

No matter how difficult the captain made it.

Evelyn's footsteps echoed softly in the empty hallway as she made her way to the exit, the stillness of the station amplifying every detail—the subtle creak of the floorboards, the faint hum of fluorescent lights, and the occasional distant clatter of movement from somewhere deeper inside the building. She was rehearsing the next day's strategy in her mind, the focused rhythm of her thoughts keeping her stride steady.

Turning the corner with purpose, Evelyn's thoughts were already tangled in logistics and numbers, the calculations and reports that had become her constant companions since arriving in Phoenix Ridge. She barely registered the shadow of movement in her periphery before her shoulder collided with someone—someone solid and unyielding. Instinct kicked in, and she shifted just in time to avoid a full-on collision, her shoulder brushing a steady arm as she stumbled a half-step back. The contact was fleeting but electric, a jolt that seemed to light up every nerve ending.

In that split second, everything around them faded. The busy firehouse, the echo of distant voices, the fluorescent hum—it all vanished, replaced by the charged silence of the narrow hallway. Evelyn's eyes lifted, meeting Cassidy's startled gaze, and the world narrowed down to a single breath.

Cass's dark blue eyes were wide with surprise, her expression momentarily unguarded. And there was something else there, too—a glint of something raw, curiosity threaded with a challenge that seemed to cut right through Evelyn's carefully constructed composure.

She felt her heart stutter, an uninvited reaction that sent a surge of heat through her. This was just Cassidy Harris, she told herself, the same stubborn fire captain who had argued with her over every point in that meeting. But standing this close, Evelyn felt her own practiced calm slipping, her pulse kicking into an unsteady rhythm. She'd faced down politicians, CEOs, critics—all without blinking. Yet here she was, in the hallway of a firehouse, rendered breathless by a look.

"Apologies, Captain," she managed, her voice sounding steadier than she felt. She took a small step back, putting an inch of space between them as she forced herself to exhale. Her hand twitched at her side, itching to dispel the lingering warmth from that brief touch, but she resisted the impulse, letting her fingers rest calmly at her side, even as her chest tightened.

Cassidy's surprise faded quickly, a small smirk pulling at the corners of her mouth as she tilted her head, an acknowledgment as much as it was a silent dare. "No harm done," she replied, her tone low, the words rougher, almost intimate in the confined space. They echoed in the hallway, filling the narrow gap between them with a pulse of something hot and alive. Cassidy's gaze lingered on her, a spark of intrigue flickering beneath her steady exterior.

And that look—it unsettled Evelyn more than she wanted to admit. Cassidy's stare wasn't filled with the polite professionalism she was accustomed to nor even the guarded hostility from their earlier meetings. There was something piercing and hungry in it, something that both unnerved and thrilled her, a challenge that reached beyond their professional friction and into the core of her own guarded reserve.

As Cassidy stepped back, Evelyn felt the faintest brush of her scent—smoke, adrenaline, and something unmistakably earthy that clung to her like an afterthought. It lingered, even as Cassidy's tall muscular figure started down the hallway in her navy blue fire uniform, her steps confident and sure, shoulders squared with that undeniable presence. Evelyn's gaze trailed after her, unable to look away, a reluctant fascination drawing her eyes to the captain's form as she moved with an ease that bordered on grace.

What the hell was wrong with herself? Evelyn forced herself to breathe, squaring her shoulders. This wasn't like her, this flare of irrational attraction that had no place here. She was Evelyn Ford: calculating, efficient, always in control. She knew better than to let emotion interfere with her work, and yet, here she was, unsettled by a fire captain who seemed to be every bit her opposite. Cassidy Harris was infuriating and stubborn, always so certain of her own way of doing things. So why did Evelyn's skin still prickle from that single accidental touch?

Get a grip, Evelyn. She forced herself to focus, to shove the thought down, to file it away as some fluke of chemistry or stress. It didn't matter. But as she turned away, heading for the exit, the hallway suddenly felt too narrow, the air charged and suffocating. She'd built her career on objectivity, on keeping everything perfectly measured and controlled. The last thing she needed was this disruption, this...unpredictable, unfamiliar distraction.

As she walked out into the cool night air, she hoped it would clear her head. She took a long, steadying breath, but the ghost of Cassidy's gaze stayed with her, lingering beneath her skin like an unwelcome thrill, a reminder of the unexpected spark that flared in that brief moment.

Evelyn paused, pressing her fingertips to her temple, as if that might erase the memory. But she couldn't shake the way Cassidy had looked at her, the weight of that moment. No, this was just another job, another clash of wills in a career built on making hard decisions. She repeated that to herself, hoping it would sink in, hoping it would smother the unnerving flicker of heat that had ignited in Cassidy's presence.

But somewhere deep down, she knew this was different. And that, more than anything, made her uneasy.

Evelyn settled into the driver's seat, the car's interior quiet except for the faint ticking of the cooling engine. The silence seemed to wrap around her like a shroud, muting the lingering hum of the evening's encounter. She let out a slow breath, the movement shallow, as though exhaling too deeply might break whatever thin hold she had on her composure.

Her eyes drifted to the station, the warm glow spilling out into the dark street, the figures moving behind frosted glass that seemed worlds apart from her. It was strange, almost infuriating, how Cassidy Harris managed to unsettle her. She'd faced tougher opposition in boardrooms and across negotiation tables, leaders with hardened gazes and iron-fisted control over their domains. But there was something different about Harris. The way she carried herself, the silent pledge she seemed to make to everyone around her—it wasn't just leadership; it was loyalty personified.

Why should that matter? Evelyn's jaw clenched as she turned the thought over. She reminded herself that her job had never been personal. Her role was to bring efficiency, to cut through the tangled web of outdated practices with precise, uncompromising changes. Phoenix Ridge Fire Department was no different. Cassidy Harris was just another piece on the board, a player in the push and pull she'd grown accustomed to.

But then why did she linger in my mind? The question pressed in uninvited, and Evelyn's fingers tightened on the steering wheel, the knuckles paling. She told herself it was the thrill of challenge, the friction of meeting resistance that made her pulse spike. There was no other explanation, no deeper reason. Cassidy's blue eyes, fierce and searching, and the fleeting touch of her big strong hand—it was all circumstantial, nothing more.

Evelyn shifted in her seat and looked at her reflection in the rearview mirror. The face staring back at her was controlled, each line familiar, each expression rehearsed. She gave herself a sharp nod, as if cementing her resolve. Tomorrow, she would start implementing the first phase of changes, no matter how many unspoken promises hung in the air or how many challenging stares met her across the table. Cass Harris was formidable, yes, but Evelyn knew how to manage resistance, how to turn it into a tool for her success.

A flicker of light caught her eye as the fire station bay doors closed, sealing off the warm, chaotic life inside. She shifted the car into gear, the low hum of the engine cutting through the silence. The station's lights blurred and then disappeared in the rearview mirror, and Evelyn's expression returned to its practiced calm, the armor she always wore.

But even as the road stretched ahead, dark and lined with the promise of order she would bring, her fingers flexed unconsciously on the wheel. The echo of Cass's stare, that searing moment where their hands brushed pulsed just beneath the surface. With a deliberate exhale, Evelyn pushed it away, eyes fixed forward and mind reset.

It was nothing, she told herself. An anomaly, irrelevant to the mission. And as the city lights of Phoenix Ridge swallowed her up, Evelyn made sure the hint of a smirk never touched her lips, no matter how stubbornly the memory tried to intrude.

3

CASS

Cass sat at her cluttered desk in the modest office of the firehouse, the morning sun spilling through the window and casting a warm glow over the stacks of reports and the mementos of past calls that adorned her workspace. A framed photo of her team at last year's annual gala stood prominently, smiles wide and arms slung around each other in a camaraderie forged in the heat of battle and the warmth of friendship. It was a comforting sight, a reminder of her purpose as she prepared for another busy day.

The sharp trill of the phone broke the

calm, and she reached for it instinctively, her heart lifting as she recognized the number.

"Chief Thompson!" Cass exclaimed, the name spilling from her lips like a long-lost song, her voice carrying both excitement and nostalgia.

"Cass! Sunshine and waves here. It's absolutely gorgeous!" Becky's voice poured through the receiver, bright and teasing, like a splash of warmth from the past. Cass could almost see her former chief, stretched out on a beach chair, sunglasses glinting under the sun, a faint laugh line crinkling around her eyes.

"Lucky you! What are you up to?" Cass asked, leaning back in her chair. A smile tugged at her lips as she settled into the warmth of Becky's familiar tone, feeling the stress of her day begin to ease.

"Oh, you know, just enjoying retirement," Becky replied, the sound of waves in the background making it clear she was living out her dream. "Lucinda's out snorkeling—I swear, she's part fish—and I'm just catching some rays. You wouldn't believe the colors here, Cass. The water's like glass, turquoise, and teal, as if someone splashed a postcard across the whole ocean!"

"Sounds perfect," Cass said with a wistful sigh. "You deserve every bit of it, you know. A little sunshine therapy after years of putting out literal and figurative fires."

"Oh, I'm enjoying every second," Becky said with a warm chuckle. "But enough about me. How's my favorite fire captain holding up? What's new in Phoenix Ridge?"

Cass's smile faded a bit as she considered how much had changed since Becky left. "Well, it's been interesting, to say the least. We've got a city consultant coming in. Evelyn Ford. She's here to shake things up and cut costs, and the team isn't exactly thrilled about it."

Becky let out a sympathetic hum. "I know her type. Efficiency experts, all about numbers and graphs, right? They walk in with binders full of ideas and little understanding of what actually keeps a team running."

"Exactly. The team is nervous—and, if I'm being honest, I am too." Cass ran a hand over her forehead, the weight of the past few days pressing down on her. "The department's got its quirks, but we all work together like family. Evelyn just...she doesn't get that. She sees us as numbers to rearrange."

"She's probably like most consultants," Becky said, a gentle caution in her voice. "She'll push her own agenda hard, maybe even in ways that get under your skin. But here's the thing, Cass. You're the one who knows Phoenix Ridge. You know its strengths and challenges better than anyone. She might have her spreadsheets, but you have their loyalty. That's something no report can capture."

Cass nodded, finding comfort in Becky's words. "I just don't want the team to lose what makes us...us. We've worked hard to build a culture of trust, where everyone's got each other's backs. I'm worried that if I push back too hard, she'll think I'm refusing to cooperate."

"Don't let her mistake your strength for resistance," Becky advised, her tone steady but encouraging. "You're in a position to stand your ground and protect what matters. Change is inevitable, but you get to control the direction it takes. If she's there to improve things, show her how things can be better without tearing down the spirit you've built."

Cass was quiet for a moment, letting Becky's words sink in. "It's just...I'm not used to feeling this defensive," she admitted, the vulnerability surprising even herself. "And it's more than just work. Evelyn, she's...well, let's just say she has a way of getting under my skin in ways I can't even explain."

"Ah," Becky chuckled knowingly. "Sounds like there's more to her than just budgets and efficiency reports."

Cass shifted uncomfortably, a laugh escaping her. "Let's just say our interactions have been complicated. It's not like me to let someone get to me this way, but she challenges me and not just in a professional sense. I can't tell if I'm frustrated or intrigued."

"Maybe both?" Becky offered with a laugh. "Sometimes the people who challenge us the most are the ones who make us grow. But be careful, Cass. If she's here to stay for a while, make sure whatever this is doesn't throw you off balance. You're the captain, and they're looking to you."

Cass straightened, feeling Becky's unwavering belief in her, and for a moment, the storm of emotions she'd been carrying settled. "You're right, Becky. I need to remember that. This department isn't just a job to me. It's my family, and I have to put that first, no matter what she brings."

Becky's voice softened, carrying that familiar warmth that always steadied Cass. "Trust yourself, Cass. Phoenix Ridge couldn't have a better leader. The team will follow where you lead, especially if they see you standing up for them."

Cass smiled, feeling the knot of tension in her chest begin to loosen. "Thanks, Becky. I needed this talk. I just have to trust myself and know I can navigate this without letting her push me into a corner."

"Exactly. Show her your strength and your heart, and remind her what Phoenix Ridge is built on. And remember, Cass, you're not just standing up to her; you're standing up for your team. There's a difference."

Cass felt a renewed sense of purpose settle over her. "I will. Thanks, Becky. For everything. Go enjoy those waves for me."

Playing with Fire

"Oh, I plan to! And remember, if you ever need a beach getaway to clear your head, I've got a chair waiting here with your name on it."

Cass laughed, feeling lighter than she had in days. "I'll hold you to that. Give my love to Lucinda."

"I will. Now go show that consultant what Phoenix Ridge Fire Department is made of."

As Cass hung up, Becky's words echoed in her mind, filling her with strength. Whatever came next, she was ready.

As they wrapped up the conversation, Cass hung up the phone, feeling a surge of confidence. But as the quiet of the station enveloped her once more, a flicker of doubt crept in. Her mind slipped back to the hallway encounter with Evelyn—the way their arms had brushed, the intensity in Evelyn's gaze, the strange electric energy that had ignited between them.

Why can't I shake this feeling? Cass frowned, the memory gnawing at her. She stood and looked out the window, the sun warming her face, but the unease lingered like a shadow, refusing to dissipate in the light. She took a deep breath, pushing the thoughts aside for now. With Becky's words echoing in her mind, Cass resolved to focus on her team and the challenges ahead.

∼

The main meeting room of the firehouse felt heavier than usual, an air of tension clinging to the walls like smoke from a recent blaze. The department heads sat around a well-worn table, its surface cluttered with spreadsheets and budget reports, the stark reality of finances hanging over them like a dark cloud. Cass glanced at the clock, feeling the weight of anticipation settle in her stomach, mentally preparing for the clash that was sure to come.

The door swung open, and Evelyn strode in, her posture immaculate and commanding, a clipboard in hand that seemed like an extension of her authority. Her shiny blonde wavy hair was as perfect as ever. Cass felt the immediate spark of tension as their eyes met for a brief moment—an electric connection that sent a jolt through the air.

"Let's get started," Evelyn said, her voice

cool and clipped as she took her seat at the head of the table, her gaze sweeping the room. She exuded a practiced composure that seemed to put an invisible barrier between herself and everyone else in the room.

As the meeting commenced, Evelyn laid out her plan for budget cuts with a crisp efficiency that left little room for debate. "We need to streamline our resources," she stated, each word calculated and precise. "This will allow us to focus on core operations and enhance overall efficiency. With the current economic climate, we can't afford to be sentimental or wasteful."

Cass leaned forward, barely containing her frustration. She could feel the team's eyes on her, waiting for her response. "But at what cost?" she challenged, her tone steady but carrying an undeniable heat. "These changes are going to hit morale hard, and we can't just reduce everything to numbers. This department relies on trust and camaraderie. You take that away, and you're left with people who don't feel valued or safe."

Evelyn's gaze flickered, a slight crease forming in her brow as she leaned forward, meeting Cass's eyes head-on. "I understand that, Captain Harris, but you have to consider the bigger picture. If we're bogged down with unnecessary expenses, it limits our ability to invest in better equipment or more training, things that directly improve safety and service outcomes. Efficiency isn't just a buzzword; it's essential for the sustainability of this department."

Cass felt a pulse of irritation at Evelyn's unflinching tone. "With all due respect, Evelyn, I think you're underestimating the human side of this. The equipment is important, yes, but it's the people who make it work. We've been able to handle emergencies with what we have because we trust each other and know our strengths. Strip away that support, and you're left with a department running on fumes."

Evelyn sighed, shifting in her seat slightly, though her expression remained resolute. "I'm not here to diminish the hard work of your team, Captain. But it's my job to ensure the department's financial viability. If we're weighed down by excess spending on non-essential services, we won't have the resources to invest in what actually keeps everyone safe."

Cass's jaw tightened, her voice a touch sharper. "And who defines what's essential? I've been in those fires, Evelyn. I've seen what happens when corners are cut—seen firefighters struggle with outdated gear or lack of support because someone, somewhere decided it wasn't essential. You can't put a price on people's lives or the trust we've build here."

Evelyn's eyes narrowed just slightly, but her tone remained measured. "Cass, it's precisely because I care about safety that I'm pushing for these changes. I'm not suggesting we take away anything crucial to your team's survival. I'm advocating for adjustments that'll let us redistribute funds to things that matter even more. Better equipment, updated training, facilities—resources that will ultimately serve your team better."

Cass folded her arms, sitting back in her chair with a skeptical look. "And how much of this decision-making comes from actually understanding the work we do here? Or is it all about reading numbers on paper? This team, this department—it's more than just a list of expenses to rearrange."

Evelyn's expression softened momentarily, though she held her ground. "Look, I respect what you do, Cass. But we're not talking about getting rid of teamwork or trust. I understand those intangibles matter, but if we don't bring this department up to speed in terms of resources, we're looking at a slow decline. And as much as I'd like to preserve everything that makes your team what it is, we have to make sacrifices for the greater good."

Cass felt her frustration deepen, her voice sharpening. "Sacrifices? This is our lives, our routines. You're asking people who put themselves on the line every day to take on even more risk, all in the name of 'efficiency.' You can't just put that on paper and call it progress."

The two women locked eyes, the tension in the room thickening as their stances crystallized. Evelyn spoke with finality, her voice low but firm. "Progress isn't easy, and it's rarely painless. But it's my job to ensure this department survives, not just this year, but years down the line. That's my priority."

Cass leaned forward, meeting Evelyn's intensity with her own. "And mine is to make sure my team is protected right now, not just theoretically. They deserve to feel secure, not like they're at the mercy of a spreadsheet. If you want their respect, maybe you should start by showing them you value their reality, not just an ideal version of what you think it should be."

A silence fell over the room, heavy and charged, as each woman held her ground, neither willing to back down.

The debate escalated, both women leaning into the conversation, their voices low yet intense, each point reverberating off the walls like a challenge thrown in the ring. Cass felt the heat of their argument, a fierce energy crackling between them as they navigated the complex terrain of budgets and personal convictions.

In a moment of movement, Cass reached for a document, and their arms brushed against one another—a fleeting touch, but it felt electric. Her pulse quickened, the contact igniting a strange awareness that sent a wave of heat coursing through her veins. Time seemed to freeze as they both registered the connection, the air thickening with unspoken tension.

The conversation faltered, their eyes

locking for a heartbeat longer than necessary. Cass felt a magnetic pull, an intoxicating draw that made her heart race as she realized Evelyn was standing just a bit too close. The world around them narrowed until it was just the two of them in that charged space. Evelyn's gaze flickered to Cass's lips, and for a brief moment, the argument faded into the background, replaced by something raw and compelling.

But just as the air seemed to vibrate with possibility, the sharp blare of the station's alarm shattered the moment, cutting through the tension like a fire hose slicing through flames. The sound was urgent, demanding attention, and the spell was broken.

Cass instinctively stepped back, breaking eye contact, her mind racing as she processed the sudden shift from intimacy to urgency. The room erupted into action as everyone sprang from their seats, adrenaline kicking in as the reality of their jobs took precedence over the personal sparks that had flared moments before.

Cass moved with the fluid urgency of a practiced leader, her heart still racing as she mentally shook off the weight of what had

Playing with Fire 55

just transpired. The memory of that fleeting touch lingered, a ghost in the chaos as they prepared to respond to the emergency call. As she grabbed her gear, Cass cast a quick glance at Evelyn, who stood frozen for a fraction of a second, clipboard clutched tightly. Their eyes met again, but this time there was no time for hesitation—only the fierce commitment to their duties, even as the tension between them continued to smolder beneath the surface.

∽

The energy in the firehouse shifted as the alarm blared, urgency sparking a flurry of movement. Cass quickly gathered her gear, her heart pounding not just from the impending call but from the charged encounter with Evelyn that still lingered in her mind. The adrenaline coursed through her veins, heightening her senses as she shouted commands to her team.

"Let's move! Gear up, everyone!" Cass called, her voice cutting through the chaos. The familiar rhythm of teamwork fell into place as firefighters donned their jackets and helmets, the camaraderie fueling her resolve. Each person moved with purpose, the sound of zippers and clanking gear a comforting backdrop against the uncertainty of the call ahead.

As they rushed toward the trucks, Cass could feel the buzz of excitement and adrenaline blending with the lingering tension from the meeting. She stole a quick glance back at Evelyn, who stood framed in the doorway, her expression unreadable. Evelyn's eyes met Cass's, and in that moment, it felt as though time slowed again, the world around them fading into a blur.

Cass swallowed hard, the mix of frustration and anticipation swirling inside her. There was something about Evelyn—something that drew her in even as it irritated her. The conversation they had shared, the brush of their arms, the heat in the air; it was all replaying in her mind like a highlight reel of a game she couldn't quite win.

"Let's go!" Cass urged, shaking off the feeling as she hopped into the passenger seat of the fire truck, her focus shifting to the task at hand. The engine roared to life, and the siren wailed, cutting through the thick air of the firehouse as the truck rumbled forward.

As they pulled away, Cass took one last look at Evelyn, standing alone in the doorway, her stance a mix of professionalism and something more elusive. There was a hardness to her expression, a determination that mirrored Cass's own resolve, and for a moment, Cass felt the weight of the unknown looming ahead.

The fire truck sped down the street, the familiar sounds of the city blurring past them. Cass clenched the handle of the door, her mind racing with thoughts of the fire they were headed to and the complex dynamics evolving within her department. Whatever had just happened with Evelyn was far from over; it was an unspoken challenge lingering in the air, and Cass was determined to face it head-on.

"Focus, Cass," she muttered under her breath, redirecting her attention to her crew and the urgency of their mission.

Cass gripped the door handle tighter, her knuckles turning white as the siren screamed overhead, cutting through the air like a knife. The team sat behind her, focused and quiet, preparing for the call ahead—a reported house fire on the edge of town. She should have been thinking about the logistics: the hydrant placement, the best approach to contain the flames, the safety of her team. And yet, her mind kept circling back to Evelyn Ford. Shiny blonde wavy hair. Intense grey eyes. Elegance personified.

Damn her.

The woman had been in her life for barely a week, and already she was under Cass's skin. Evelyn was everything Cass hated—cold, calculated, and with that ridiculous clipboard always in hand, ready to slash budgets and strip resources from the people who needed them most. She had a knack for asking pointed questions that felt more like accusations, and her clipped tone grated on Cass like sandpaper. Cass had fought tooth and nail for this department, and Evelyn acted like it was just another line item in her ledger.

And yet...

Cass's jaw tightened as they turned down the main road, the truck's engine roaring beneath her. And yet, every time Evelyn spoke, Cass couldn't help but notice the sharp intelligence in her ice grey eyes, the way her words cut straight to the heart of the matter. There was a fire in Evelyn, too, one Cass hadn't expected. It wasn't the same as the camaraderie Cass shared with her crew or the burning passion for saving lives that had defined her career. Evelyn's fire was different—controlled, deliberate, like the steady burn of a forge.

It pissed Cass off to no end.

Because she shouldn't be noticing things like that. She shouldn't be wondering what Evelyn looked like when she let that icy control crack, shouldn't be replaying their arguments in her head like some kind of masochistic ritual. She hated Evelyn Ford. Hated the way she barged into their station with her spreadsheets and her condescending smirks, hated the way she dismissed years of tradition with a few carefully chosen words.

But most of all, she hated the way Evelyn made her feel.

The heat that curled low in her stomach whenever their eyes locked across the room. The way her pulse quickened, not just with anger, but with something else—something she couldn't name and didn't want to examine too closely. It was infuriating. She had no business feeling anything for Evelyn Ford except contempt.

"Captain, we're almost there," Hallie Hunter's voice cut through her thoughts, jolting her back to the present.

Cass nodded, shaking her head as though she could dislodge the thoughts tangled up inside it. Focus, she told herself. There was a fire to fight, a family to save. This was what mattered, not some infuriating consultant with a sharp tongue and a perfectly pressed suit.

She pushed Evelyn out of her mind. Or tried to, anyway. But as the house came into view, its roof already engulfed in flames, Cass couldn't help the nagging thought that the fire raging inside her was just as dangerous.

4

EVELYN

The fire station hummed with energy as firefighters bustled around, prepping for the day's routine drill. The scent of fresh coffee mingled with the faint whiff of smoke and the metallic tang of equipment, creating a familiar backdrop for the team. Laughter echoed off the walls as firefighters exchanged playful banter, their camaraderie evident in the way they moved together like a well-oiled machine. Both Captains Harris and Hunter's teams ran the drills today, competing for the best times. Evelyn had watched the interactions between Cass and Hallie over the last few days.

Captain Hallie Hunter seemed to be a calming influence on the fiery captain Harris, settling her when tensions ran high and emotions flared. Perhaps she ought to be spending her attention there instead of Harris; it would be a much easier fight. But then she did so enjoy the challenge.

Evelyn stepped through the double doors, clipboard in hand, her presence commanding immediate attention. The clamor faded momentarily as she surveyed the scene with a critical eye. The light streaming through the high windows illuminated the dust motes swirling in the air, but her focus was on the equipment scattered around the bay. Old hoses lay coiled in a corner, a couple ladders showed signs of wear, and the fire engines looked like they had seen better days.

She noted each deficiency, her brow furrowing deeper with every observation. In her mind, a plan began to form: more budget cuts would allow her to advocate for new gear and better safety measures for the department, streamlining their operations to meet modern standards. Efficiency, she reminded herself, was key to their survival.

As she moved to the edge of the drill area, Evelyn felt the palpable sense of pride and teamwork among the firefighters. They communicated effortlessly, their movements synchronized as they checked equipment and briefed one another on their roles for the drill. She couldn't deny the camaraderie on display—the way they rallied together, their faces alight with purpose and determination.

But even as she acknowledged their spirit, her focus remained unwaveringly on the deficiencies she perceived. The outdated equipment loomed larger in her mind, overshadowing the warmth of their interactions. She scribbled notes furiously, capturing every detail, every potential point of improvement, and the nagging feeling that some of the traditions held dear were standing in the way of progress.

Evelyn watched as Cass Harris barked orders, her voice rising above the noise, commanding respect from her team. There was a fire in Cass that Evelyn found both admirable and infuriating. How could a department this proud and capable be content with equipment that had clearly seen better days?

She had researched a lot of the most up to date firefighting equipment and they had none of it here. She would have to confront Cass about it—and soon.

As the drill began, Evelyn stood back, arms crossed, keenly observing the execution from the women. The routine unfolded with precision, but all she could see were the gaps, the places where they could improve. She felt the weight of her mission pressing down on her, ready to advocate for the changes she believed were necessary to secure the department's future.

With every passing moment, her resolve hardened, but she couldn't shake the sense that the real challenge wasn't just the equipment; it was going to be navigating the complex dynamics within this fiercely loyal team.

∼

After the drill concluded, Evelyn gathered the team in the main meeting room, her clipboard at the ready, the atmosphere thick with anticipation. The walls, adorned with plaques and photos of past achievements,

Playing with Fire 65

seemed to close in as the team settled into their seats, their expressions shifting from camaraderie to seriousness. Cass entered last, her presence commanding, but a flicker of tension danced in the air between her and Evelyn.

Evelyn cleared her throat, casting a steady gaze around the room before settling on Cass. "Thank you all for your hard work today," she began, her voice calm yet firm. "I wanted to take a moment to go over a few critical observations from the drill." Her eyes flicked over the team, but eventually rested on Cass, whose arms were crossed defensively, her expression guarded yet intent.

"While I commend your dedication, it's clear that some of the equipment is outdated," Evelyn continued, letting the words hang in the air. "If you want to operate efficiently and safely, we need to consider reallocating funds for new tools."

Cass's expression immediately tightened and her blue eyes narrowed at "outdated" and "reallocate." She sat up straighter and her jaw clenched, the tension evident in the set of her shoulders. Her dark ponytail was messy from her helmet. "Evelyn, I hear what you're saying, but this equipment has served us for years. It's not shiny or new, but it's reliable and we know how to handle it." Her voice was steady, but there was an edge there, a warning. "We've made do with what we have, and we've done it successfully. Just because it's not top of the line doesn't mean it's ineffective."

Evelyn's gaze sharpened, and she shook her head, unfazed. "But you're not seeing the bigger picture, Cass," she replied, her voice growing firmer. "The field is changing rapidly. We can't fall behind while other departments are modernizing their equipment and practices. Adaptation is essential if we want to stay at the forefront of fire safety and rescue. Budget cuts to certain areas would allow us to prioritize new resources for the future."

Cass's expression darkened, her patience wearing thin. She leaned forward, her tone sharpening with each word. "You think you can just waltz in here and tell us what we need without really understanding our team? This isn't just about gear or a budget line, Evelyn. It's about who we are and what we stand for. These tools aren't just equipment to us—they're trusted, battle-tested, and every firefighter here knows them like the back of their hand. You can't just come in and start dismantling that trust."

Evelyn's brows knit together as she took a step closer, meeting Cass's challenge head-on. "I understand the history and traditions here, but clinging to old tools and old ways just because they're comfortable isn't an option. I'm here to make sure we're prioritizing safety and effectiveness over sentimentality. You may see it as dismantling trust, but I see it as building resilience, ensuring that every single person on this team has the best chance to come out of a fire alive."

Cass's eyes narrowed, and she rose from her seat, now fully facing Evelyn, their proximity shrinking as the air between them thickened with tension. Her voice dropped, low but fierce. "Don't talk to me about resilience. You don't get resilience by handing over shiny new tools every time there's a budget cut somewhere else. You get it by investing in the people who use those tools day in and day out, who've put in hours learning to trust their equipment and each other. This team isn't a line item. We're not numbers on a spreadsheet."

Evelyn felt her pulse quicken as Cass moved closer, her words striking a nerve that she hadn't expected. She straightened, matching Cass's defiance, refusing to back down. "I'm not here to turn you into numbers. I'm here to make sure that your team can keep up with the demands of the job and handle the next crisis without hesitation. Cutting costs now means we can save lives tomorrow, Cass. We can't afford to treat this like it's a question of loyalty or tradition. This is about efficiency and strategy."

Cass's hands clenched at her sides, her voice simmering with frustration. "Efficiency and strategy? Evelyn, firefighting isn't a business plan. You can't put a price on the trust my crew has built with the tools they use every day. And you can't quantify the spirit of this department on a spreadsheet. You may think you know what's best for us, but you're underestimating what makes this team strong."

Evelyn's jaw tightened as she took another step forward, her voice just above a whisper but charged with intensity. "I'm not underestimating anything, Cass. I'm trying to prepare your department for the future. Do you know how many firehouses have gone under because they refused to adapt? I have seen it. It starts with a reluctance to change, and it ends with lives lost that could have been saved if only they had been willing to move forward."

The room seemed to shrink around them as they stood toe-to-toe, each holding their ground with unwavering conviction. Cass's voice was barely a breath, but the intensity was unmistakable. "You talk about lives, but you don't understand what it takes to walk into a burning building and trust that everything you're holding on to won't fail you. You don't know what it's like to bet your life on a piece of equipment that isn't just new and unfamiliar but hasn't been field-tested with your team beside you."

Evelyn's eyes flashed, and she stepped in even closer, nearly brushing against Cass's chest as her own voice dropped to match the ferocity of the moment. "And you don't know what it's like to see preventable tragedies because people were too proud to make the necessary changes. Tradition doesn't save lives, Cass. It's time to look beyond comfort and think about survival, not just for the next fire but for the next decade."

They were so close now that Evelyn could see the fire in Cass's brilliant blue eyes, a wild determination mixed with something deeper, a spark that went beyond their professional clash. She was sure Cass could feel her own heartbeat racing in her chest. Neither moved, neither spoke, each holding the tension in the space between them, a crackling friction that seemed to blur the line between fury and something else.

Finally, Cass's voice dropped to a growl, her gaze unwavering. "This team is my family, Evelyn. I won't stand by while you reduce them to some numbers on a line graph."

Evelyn's response came just as low, her voice tight. "I'm not here to destroy your family, Cass. I'm here to make sure they stay alive."

For a moment, it felt as though the words between them weren't just about policy or funding or even safety. The unspoken tension in their heated exchange held something raw and electric. Their breaths mingled, and

Evelyn felt a shiver she couldn't deny, her pulse pounding in her ears as she stood inches from Cass, the intensity of their argument eclipsed only by the unbidden pull she felt toward her.

Just as Cass was about to respond, the air between them shifted, thickening with an electric charge that hung heavily. Cass leaned in just a fraction closer, and Evelyn's heart raced, caught in the moment as their faces neared. But then, suddenly, a reality check jolted through Evelyn. She pulled back, her composure barely intact.

The tension lingered in the air, charged and unresolved, leaving both women rattled. Cass's jaw clenched, a mixture of frustration and determination etched on her features, while Evelyn felt the heat of the argument mix with an inexplicable connection that left her unnerved.

The team remained silent, sensing the crackling tension, waiting for either woman to break the stalemate. Evelyn took a deep breath, steadied herself, and steered the conversation back to the budget, but the encounter had irrevocably changed the dynamics of their relationship, leaving both women acutely aware of the boundaries they had just tested.

~

Evelyn settled back into her office, the familiar surroundings doing little to soothe the turbulent thoughts swirling in her mind. The polished desk, adorned with neatly stacked reports and strategic plans, felt cluttered by the memories of the heated argument with Cass. She glanced at the papers, but they blurred together as her focus drifted back to the firehouse, to Cass's fierce eyes blazing with passion igniting something within her that she hadn't anticipated.

The image replayed in her mind: Cass standing firm, her unwavering resolve practically radiating from her. Evelyn couldn't shake the way Cass had leaned in, their faces mere inches apart, the air thick with unspoken tension. It was a confrontation that had shifted something within her, and the realization rattled her more than she cared to admit.

Evelyn had always been prepared for opposition. It was part of her job, part of the game she had mastered. But Cass was different. Her fervor struck a chord deep inside, a mix of irritation and intrigue that left Evelyn feeling uncharacteristically unsettled. She had faced stubbornness before, but this was a challenge wrapped in something she couldn't quite define, something magnetic that pulled at her, even as she tried to distance herself from it.

With a frustrated sigh, Evelyn leaned back in her chair, running a hand through her hair. "Focus," she murmured to herself, trying to push the distraction away. She glanced at her to-do list, mentally sorting through the tasks at hand. Budget cuts. New proposals. Strategy meetings. Each item felt weightier than before, as if Cass's passionate defiance had seeped into every facet of her work.

She attempted to dive back into her notes, but her mind kept wandering back to the firehouse. The way Cass had stood her ground, the spark of challenge in her eyes—it was captivating, and it gnawed at her resolve. How could she be thinking about this? She was here to implement changes, not get caught up in personal dynamics.

"Get a grip, Evelyn," she scolded herself, attempting to rationalize her reaction. It had to be the stress of the job, the pressure of navigating an unyielding department. Surely that was it. She was simply feeling the weight of the task ahead, the challenges she had yet to face.

But no matter how hard she tried to shake it off, the connection she had felt during their argument refused to fade. It lingered like a shadow, creeping into her thoughts and complicating her focus. Each time she closed her eyes, she could see Cass's fiery expression, hear her passionate voice, and feel the tension that crackled in the air between them.

Evelyn cursed under her breath, the irritation bubbling within her. This was not who she was—she was a consultant, a strategist, a woman who thrived on clear boundaries and professionalism. Yet the memory of Cass Harris, with all her stubbornness, defied that neat categorization, complicating the very essence of what it meant to be resolute.

As the afternoon sun dipped lower outside her office window, casting long shadows

Playing with Fire

across her desk, Evelyn knew she needed to regain control. She opened her laptop, determined to immerse herself in her work, to drown out the persistent thoughts of Cass and the unexpected draw that simmered beneath the surface. But as she typed, the words blurred again, overshadowed by a single truth: the tension between them was far from over, and Evelyn had a feeling it was only the beginning.

Evelyn sat by the window, the warm glow of the setting sun casting a golden hue over her office. The light danced across her paperwork, illuminating the stacks of reports and proposals that filled her desk. Yet despite the chaos of her surroundings, her mind was a whirlpool of thoughts focused entirely on the challenge that lay ahead.

She gazed out at the horizon, where the fiery colors of dusk blended together, much like the tumultuous emotions swirling within her. Cass's fiery spirit and the palpable tension of their last encounter replayed in her mind, a mix of exhilaration and trepidation. Evelyn took a deep breath, letting the cool air fill her lungs. She straightened in her chair, rolling her shoulders back and settling into the confidence she had worked so hard to cultivate. *Focus on the mission,* she told herself, her gaze dropping to the array of spreadsheets and notes scattered across her desk. Efficiency, modernization, cost-cutting—these were the tenets of her role, the foundation of the task she'd been assigned. She wasn't here to indulge sentimentality; she was here to enact change.

Her pen tapped against the desk as she reviewed her thoughts, honing the argument she would bring to the table at her next meeting with Captain Cass Harris. The woman was a walking embodiment of stubbornness and emotion, her fiery passion for the department radiating from every word and gesture. Evelyn had to admit, albeit grudgingly, that Cass's dedication was impressive. But it was also deeply misguided.

Sentiment doesn't keep the lights on or the equipment running, Evelyn thought with a sharpness that surprised even herself. Cass could wax poetic all she wanted about the "family" the department represented, but Evelyn knew the reality. Without funding and fiscal responsibility, that family would collapse under the weight of its own inefficiencies. Cass's refusal to see reason wasn't just frustrating; it was dangerous.

Evelyn leaned forward, her hands clasped on the desk as she stared at the notes before her. Every proposed change she'd brought up so far had been met with resistance from Cass. Not thoughtful questions or constructive criticism—no, that would be too reasonable. Instead, it was always fire and fury, an unrelenting pushback against anything that threatened the traditional ways of the department.

Evelyn frowned, the memory of their last meeting flashing through her mind. Cass had stood there, arms crossed, her sharp tone underpinned by an unshakable defiance. "You're not going to fix something that isn't broken, Ms. Ford," she had said, her voice carrying the weight of years of hard-earned respect within her team. Evelyn had matched her tone, of course, but the clash had left her bristling with irritation. Cass didn't seem to understand that this wasn't a debate. Evelyn wasn't there to negotiate; she was there to fix things.

The problem was Cass's reliance on emotion. Evelyn didn't doubt that Cass cared deeply for her team, but caring didn't pay bills. Loyalty didn't replace outdated equipment. And as noble as Cass's sense of responsibility was, it clouded her judgment. The fire service was supposed to be a system, a machine that operated smoothly and efficiently. Cass treated it like a fragile heirloom to be preserved at all costs.

Evelyn exhaled sharply, her jaw tightening. She didn't have time to indulge such sentimentality. Cass might see Evelyn as some kind of villain—a heartless bureaucrat sweeping in to destroy everything she'd built—but Evelyn saw herself as something else entirely: a realist. She was the one tasked with ensuring the department's survival, even if it meant dismantling the outdated practices that Cass clung to so desperately. And if Cass couldn't see that? Well, that wasn't Evelyn's problem.

Her mind churned as she began drafting her approach for the next meeting. She needed to remain firm, unmoving. Cass's fiery outbursts were designed to bait her, to pull her into emotional waters where Evelyn knew she wouldn't swim well. But she wouldn't let that happen. Not again.

You're here to do a job, Evelyn reminded herself. *Not to make friends.* It didn't matter if Cass didn't like her. In fact, Evelyn almost preferred it that way. Friendship, or even mutual respect, could muddy the waters. Keeping Cass at arm's length made it easier to focus on the task at hand.

Evelyn tapped her pen against her notepad, her mind sharpening its focus on the practicalities of the situation. If Cass couldn't adapt, then she would simply have to adjust. Evelyn wasn't going to waste time trying to win her over. She'd been through this before—working with people too rooted in their ways to see the bigger picture. It was never pleasant, but it was always necessary.

Still, Evelyn couldn't entirely ignore the challenge Cass presented. There was something undeniably compelling about the captain's presence, her unwavering commitment to her team, and her ability to command attention in a way that Evelyn couldn't quite pinpoint. It wasn't charm; it was too raw for that. It was something closer to power, and

Evelyn couldn't decide if it fascinated or irritated her more.

She leaned back in her chair, crossing her arms as she thought of Cass's fierce defense of her department. It was admirable in its own way, but it was also shortsighted. Cass's attachment to the "way things have always been" was precisely the problem. Tradition was a luxury the department couldn't afford anymore. They needed innovation, not sentiment.

Evelyn picked up a stack of proposals, thumbing through them until she found the budget restructuring draft. This was the key. If she could frame the changes in a way that made them appear less disruptive—perhaps even advantageous to the team's morale—she might be able to navigate Cass's resistance. But Evelyn knew better than to expect full cooperation. Cass was too proud, too rooted in her ideals to give in without a fight.

Fine, Evelyn thought, a hint of steel hardening her resolve. If Cass wanted a fight, Evelyn would give her one. She wasn't afraid to stand her ground. The department's future depended on it, and Evelyn had no intention of losing.

She turned back to her desk, her pen moving swiftly as she adjusted her notes. The sun dipped lower in the sky, casting a golden glow over her workspace, but Evelyn barely noticed. She was already planning her next move, a strategy that would leave no room for Cass's fiery rebuttals.

Because in the end, Evelyn didn't just want to win this fight—she *needed* to.

5

CASS

The firehouse was still, quiet except for the faint hum of the vending machine down the hall and the occasional creak of the building settling into the night. Cass sat alone in the dimly lit common room, a lukewarm cup of coffee cradled between her hands. It was past midnight, the usual dead time during a shift, a rare lull when her team could get some rest before the next call.

But tonight, Cass felt anything but restful. She'd tried everything to shake the restless energy buzzing through her veins: ran through drills with the team earlier, checked equipment twice, even forced herself into paperwork she'd normally avoid. Yet her mind kept snapping back to the one thing she wanted to forget.

Evelyn Ford.

Her jaw clenched at the thought of the consultant's name, her grip tightening around the cup until the lukewarm coffee sloshed dangerously close to the rim. She'd dealt with bureaucrats before—always there to slash budgets, to dictate policies they knew nothing about—and she'd faced them down with an unwavering resolve. But Evelyn was unsettlingly different. From the moment she'd walked into Cass's firehouse with that calculated, steely gaze and a confident, almost arrogant stance, Evelyn had rattled her. More than that, Evelyn had gotten under her skin in a way Cass couldn't seem to shake.

"Focus on the job, Cass," she muttered to herself, as if speaking it aloud would somehow break the spell. But even as she tried to push the thought aside, memories from their last encounter crowded back into her mind with unnerving clarity.

She could still see Evelyn standing there, calm and unbending, going toe-to-toe with her in that heated meeting. Cass replayed every word, every subtle barb, the way Evelyn's sharp grey gaze never faltered, her coolness that felt almost like a challenge. Her shiny hair that was never a hair out of place. Cass's heart had hammered against her ribs, her pulse racing not just with frustration but with something else—something that made her skin tingle and her breath catch. She hated that her body seemed to react to Evelyn without her permission. Hated that someone who threatened everything she'd built could also ignite something within her she hadn't felt in years.

She set her coffee down and ran her hands over her face, exhaling a frustrated sigh. This wasn't like her. Cassidy Harris didn't get distracted, didn't let anyone or anything cloud her focus on her team, her work. And yet here she was, in the dead of night, haunted by Evelyn Ford's sharp, unyielding grey gaze, shiny hair, and the lovely lines of her body in her smart suits. She kept imagining what it might be like to tear those perfect clothes from her perfect body. And the thought more than excited her.

Cass leaned back against the wall of the

firehouse, the hum of the building's late-night quiet pressing in on her as she tried to clear her mind. But no matter how hard she pushed, Evelyn Ford kept slipping into her thoughts, like smoke finding its way through cracks. It was maddening, this unwelcome distraction at a time when her department needed her focus more than ever. The weight of her responsibility felt heavier tonight, almost suffocating, as she grappled with the changes Evelyn was determined to bring.

She had promised herself and, more importantly, she had promised her team that she'd do everything in her power to protect them and preserve the firehouse culture that Chief Becky Thompson had built from the ground up. Cass had spent her career in the shadow of Becky's legacy, learning from the best, witnessing firsthand how a team could become a family. Now as their captain, she knew her crew looked to her for that same stability. Yet every time she was around Evelyn, she felt that foundation shake. It wasn't just the attraction, though that alone unsettled her. It was the way Evelyn's presence seemed to make her question everything she thought she knew, every instinct she'd honed under Becky's guidance.

A nagging sense of guilt gnawed at her. Allowing herself to be distracted by Evelyn felt like a betrayal—not just to her team, but to Becky. Cass could almost hear Becky's voice in her mind, that steady, patient tone reminding her of what mattered most. Her mentor had poured her soul into this department, building it on trust and unity, values Cass was now charged with defending. And yet here she was, feeling drawn to someone who saw numbers and efficiency where Cass saw people and purpose. Allowing Evelyn to get under her skin felt like she was failing in that duty, like she was letting Becky down by not standing stronger, more unyielding.

But there was no denying it—Evelyn did get to her. Cass hated how her pulse raced in Evelyn's presence, how even in the heat of an argument, that spark was there, pulling her closer. She'd always been so sure of herself, of her purpose. Now, that certainty was blurring, leaving her feeling untethered at the exact moment her team needed her to be their anchor.

Cass straightened, fists clenching at her

sides. She'd made it this far by staying true to what mattered, by putting her crew and their safety above everything. No matter what Evelyn stirred up in her, she couldn't afford to let it weaken her resolve. Her team's future depended on her ability to stand her ground, to fight for what she knew was right. This firehouse, these people—they deserved someone who could see past the numbers, someone who wouldn't be swayed by a fleeting attraction. She had to be that person, for their sake and for Becky's.

Cass pushed back in her chair, trying to ground herself, trying to remember that she was here for her team, for her department. Evelyn's "efficiency" cuts didn't just threaten her crew's equipment; they undermined the trust and loyalty she'd worked so hard to build. But even as she mentally fortified herself with reasons to resist Evelyn, her thoughts kept drifting back to her. The woman was infuriatingly competent, every word and gesture so damn precise. The challenge she brought into Cass's world was electric, a clash of wills that made Cass's blood hum in a way she hadn't anticipated, hadn't wanted.

Standing up, Cass crossed the room, restless energy urging her to move, to walk off the tension coiling in her muscles. She paced back and forth, her boots clicking softly on the linoleum.

"This isn't just about Evelyn," she muttered, hands on her hips as if trying to talk herself out of the tangled mess of emotions. She told herself it was about her duty to protect the department and her crew, and yet every attempt to ground herself brought her right back to that moment in the meeting room—Evelyn's face inches from hers, the air crackling with something intense and forbidden.

Cass remembered the way Evelyn's gaze had softened, just for a flicker of a second before returning to that businesslike coolness. It was almost as if she had seen through the walls Cass put up, seen the fire that simmered beneath her frustration. And for one maddening, breathless moment, Cass had wanted to reach across the space between them, to break the distance with something as raw and unfiltered as the clash they'd just shared.

"Get a grip, Harris," she scolded herself,

but the words rang hollow in the empty room. How could she get a grip when her own mind seemed to betray her? When every rational thought of resistance was undercut by the undeniable pull she felt toward Evelyn Ford?

She knew she should hate her and should resent every cool, calculated suggestion Evelyn made about "efficiency" and "reallocating resources." And she did. She truly did, with every fiber of her being. But that resentment had become tangled, interwoven with a different fire, a reckless draw that left her feeling exposed and unsure.

Cass paused, resting her hands on the counter and staring down at her reflection in the polished steel. The dim lights softened her features, her eyes shadowed and intense, the lines of tension evident even to her. She'd built her entire career on being unflappable, on being the steady, reliable captain her team could count on. And yet here she was, rattled by a woman who challenged everything she thought she knew about herself.

As she looked at her own reflection, Cass could almost hear Becky's voice in her mind, that warm, familiar guidance she'd leaned on so many times before. Becky would tell her to push through, to let her instincts guide her, and to remember who she was fighting for. But that advice, that steadiness, felt different now, complicated by the mix of anger and attraction Evelyn had stirred up.

Her thoughts drifted back to the look on Evelyn's face during their last argument—the flash of heat behind her eyes, the faint tremor in her voice when Cass pushed back. She wondered if Evelyn had felt it too, that strange, almost magnetic tension. Part of Cass wanted to believe it was just her, that Evelyn hadn't noticed the spark between them. But another part—a small, dangerous part—wanted to believe that maybe Evelyn had felt the same pull, the same unspoken, forbidden energy. And that terrified her more than anything.

Cass clenched her fists, jaw tight as she fought to regain control over her thoughts. This wasn't her. She wasn't someone who lost focus, who let a woman with a clipboard and a spreadsheet shake her up. But the more she tried to bury her attraction, the more it seemed to claw its way back to the surface, relentless and insistent.

Finally, Cass grabbed her coffee and took a long, bracing sip, as if the lukewarm bitterness could snap her out of this spiral. She reminded herself, yet again, that this was just another challenge, another person trying to make changes she didn't believe in. But even as she forced herself to focus on the job, she couldn't fully ignore the way Evelyn lingered in her thoughts like a storm cloud on the horizon, dark and powerful, promising something she wasn't ready to confront.

As the night wore on, the quiet of the firehouse pressed around her, thick and heavy, and Cass knew sleep wouldn't come easily. She'd spent countless nights running over tactics and strategies, thinking through ways to strengthen her team and protect them from any risk. But tonight, her mind refused to cooperate, slipping back to Evelyn's voice, her steady, maddening gaze, and the possibility that maybe, just maybe, Cass was drawn to her not in spite of her resistance, but because of it.

With a sigh, Cass leaned back against the counter, closing her eyes for a brief moment and letting the tension wash over her. Tomorrow, she'd face Evelyn again—maybe spar, maybe clash—and try to drive a wedge between herself and the emotions she didn't want to name. But tonight, as the quiet pressed in around her, Cass allowed herself to acknowledge the truth, just for a fleeting second: Evelyn Ford had become more than just a thorn in her side; she'd become a fire, one that Cass wasn't sure she wanted to extinguish.

~

It had been a quiet night thus far, though Cass knew better than to voice such a thing aloud. Glass in hand, she returned to the silence of her office, the door closing behind her with a soft click. She flopped down onto the pullout mattress that was a fixture of the captain's office. No roughing it in the shared bunks for her these days.

God, even exhausted, she couldn't get Evelyn out of her damn mind. None of her previous fascinations or even partners had captivated her this way. In fact, that was why pretty much all of her past relationships had fizzled and died; she couldn't get her head off the job and on to them. But Evelyn had completely flipped her. The sharp staccato of her strides now played as a constant soundtrack in Cass's head. The vision of her fine, perfectly made-up hair, with the same two strands flying out of place, glistening honey highlights on the light. She couldn't kick the thought. Her voice—blunt, direct—sent needy shivers down her spine. And those perfectly manicured fingers. God, Cass could only imagine what she could do with those.

Her breathing grew shallow, and she felt her lips dry and the air around her became hot. Fuck. She shouldn't do this; not at work.

Grazing her own short nails across her chest, she caught her hardened, sensitive nipples, gasping as a spike of desire shot through her core. Tighter this time, she pinched, leaning back against the wall, her legs splayed. With a will of its own, her other hand wandered further south. Down and down until it reached the waistband of her pants. Was she really about to do this? She couldn't stop herself, even if she wanted to.

Fuck, she was already so wet by the time her rough, calloused fingers slipped between her folds. She had to stifle a moan that tried to rip through her. She couldn't make a sound. If anyone came into her office right now, she would be utterly screwed.

She was too far gone for the risk to stop her. Drawing tight circles around her clit, she replayed recent clashes with Evelyn inside her mind. Fuck, what had the woman done to her; it was like she was bewitched. She tugged harder on her nipples, pinching, squeezing, twisting, almost as though she was punishing herself for her desire. Her fingers slowly sped up until she was gasping for air, round and round they flicked across her clit, driving her wild with need. She couldn't hold it back anymore. Waves of pleasure crashed through her as she climaxed, tremors wracking her body.

Fuck.

Cass lay motionless on the pullout bed in her office, the ceiling above her dimly illuminated by the faint glow of the streetlights outside. Her breathing was still uneven, her heart pounding in her chest as the reality of what she'd just done hit her like a freight train. She squeezed her eyes shut, willing herself to sink into the mattress, to disappear entirely, as shame and self-reproach flooded her body in a tidal wave.

What the hell was wrong with her?

She rolled onto her side, burying her face in her pillow as if doing so might erase the last few minutes. But there was no escaping it. No matter how much she tried to deny it, the evidence was all there—on her skin, in the way her body still tingled with the aftershocks of release, in the name she'd bitten back in her moment of surrender. *Evelyn.*

Cass groaned into the pillow, half in anger, half in mortification. She couldn't believe she'd allowed herself to go there, to let Evelyn Ford—*Evelyn Ford*—invade her thoughts like that, consume her like a fire she couldn't put out. It wasn't just unprofessional. It was dangerous. Reckless. Everything she stood against.

The firehouse was supposed to be her sanctuary, the one place where she could focus on her responsibilities and leave everything else at the door. This office, this pullout bed—was her refuge during long nights and grueling shifts, the place where she regrouped and recharged to face whatever challenges lay ahead. And now she'd tainted it, let something slip through the cracks that never should have been there in the first place.

If anyone knew...

The thought alone made her stomach churn. Cass prided herself on being a leader her team could respect, someone they could rely on to put the job above all else. How could she look them in the eye if they knew how far she'd fallen tonight? If they even suspected that their captain, the woman who was supposed to be fighting for their future, had let herself be so thoroughly distracted by the enemy?

She sat up abruptly, swinging her legs over the side of the bed, her hands raking through her hair as if she could scrub the thoughts from her mind. But it didn't work. Evelyn was still there, vivid and unrelenting, her sharp blue eyes and infuriatingly calm demeanor etched into Cass's brain like a brand.

It wasn't just the attraction that horrified her; it was the power Evelyn seemed to have over her, the way she got under Cass's skin without even trying. Every argument, every glare, every pointed word Evelyn threw her way seemed to burrow deeper, stoking a fire that Cass had no idea how to extinguish.

And after this? She was compromised.

Cass stood, pacing the small office like a caged animal, her bare feet padding softly against the worn carpet. She needed to get a grip. She needed to shove whatever this was deep down and lock it away where it couldn't interfere with her job. Because that's what this was: interference. A distraction. A weakness that Evelyn would exploit the moment she caught wind of it.

The thought made Cass's hands clench into fists at her sides. *This can't happen again.* She couldn't afford to let it. Not with the department hanging in the balance, not with Evelyn poised to make the kind of cuts that would gut everything they'd worked so hard to build.

Her team deserved better than this. Becky Thompson had trusted her to take over, to protect this firehouse and the people who gave everything to it day after day. And here she was, betraying that trust by letting herself be consumed by someone who didn't care about their legacy, who saw the firehouse as nothing more than a line item to slash.

Cass stopped pacing, leaning heavily against her desk as she tried to catch her breath. The wood felt cool and solid beneath her hands, a stark contrast to the heat still simmering under her skin. She pressed her palms against it harder, as if grounding herself in the physical world might steady the chaos in her mind.

But even as she stood there, staring at the cluttered surface of her desk, her thoughts kept circling back to Evelyn. Not just the way she looked, the way her lips curved when she smiled, or the sharpness of her wit—but the way she challenged Cass and pushed her in ways no one else ever had. It was infuriating. It was exhilarating.

It was unacceptable.

Cass straightened, forcing her shoulders back, forcing the fire in her chest into something colder, sharper. This couldn't happen again, she told herself firmly. Tonight had been a mistake, a moment of weakness that she would bury and never revisit.

Tomorrow, she would refocus. She would throw herself into fighting for her team, and

Playing with Fire

she would treat Evelyn Ford exactly as she deserved to be treated: as an obstacle to be overcome, not a temptation to be indulged.

And if Evelyn ever looked at her again the way she had earlier that day, her eyes flickering with something unspoken, something that made Cass's pulse race against her will? Evelyn wasn't just some consultant; she was a threat. A threat to the department, to the family Cass had spent years building. If Cass so much as blinked, Evelyn could swoop in with her polished shoes and budget cuts and dismantle everything that mattered. The team wasn't just her crew; they were her people, her responsibility. Her jaw clenched as she thought of Evelyn's cold, unflinching demeanor in every meeting. The woman didn't care about what these budget cuts would do to the people behind the numbers. To Evelyn, it was all a calculation, a bottom line. Cass had seen her type before: corporate climbers who wore tailored suits and wielded spreadsheets like weapons, completely detached from the lives their decisions would destroy.

And yet...

Cass slammed her fist against the desk,

frustration boiling over. How could she *feel* this way about someone so ruthless, so devoid of compassion? What did it say about her that, despite Evelyn's apparent lack of morals, Cass couldn't stop noticing the fire behind her icy exterior?

She hated herself for it—hated the pull, the magnetic draw that kept her thoughts circling back to Evelyn. It made her feel weak, like she was failing her team by even entertaining these feelings. This wasn't her. She wasn't someone who got distracted by smooth words or sharp cheekbones.

She was Captain Cass Harris, damn it. And no one—not even Evelyn Ford—was going to tear her family apart.

Cass straightened, brushing off the tension crawling up her spine. She wouldn't let this distraction derail her. Whatever was stirring inside her, she'd bury it. Evelyn might have a spark, but Cass was a wildfire, and she'd burn this feeling to ashes before she let it consume her.

Well, Cass would just have to ignore it. Because there was no room for this. No room for *her*.

Not in Cass's firehouse. Not in her life.

6

EVELYN

The firehouse was nearly empty, the distant sounds of rustling papers and the hum of the central air filling the silence. Evelyn sat alone in the captain's office bent over a thick sheaf of budget reports. She'd been here for hours, reviewing every line item and category, recalculating figures that refused to fit into her projections. The team had been called out, and she'd taken advantage of the offer of the comfier settings than her own temporary space provided. She, of course, had her own office at the agency, but in situations like this, she preferred to have boots on the ground as such. Efficiency was supposed to be her specialty, but she hadn't expected it to feel like such a battle here. She'd given up on her usual posture, her jacket draped over the chair, and her hair was pinned back in a loose, practical knot. The air felt thick, almost stifling, as if the firehouse itself was waiting, watching her.

Papers and spreadsheets were strewn across her desk, a collection of ideas carefully compiled for her task at hand. She was determined to identify areas where the fire department could trim its budget without sacrificing safety—or so she kept telling herself. The numbers were stark, however, and her notes were peppered with tentative cuts: reducing overtime expenses, consolidating resources between neighboring departments, phasing out equipment that didn't meet the new standards. Even the possibility of closing one of the auxiliary stations in the far east part of town hovered on the edge of her considerations, though she knew the community impact would be substantial.

She tapped her pen against the page, an undercurrent of frustration simmering beneath her usual polished composure. Each suggestion seemed perfectly logical on paper, but she couldn't ignore how heavy-handed it felt, as if she were trying to disassemble a machine she barely understood. Every so often, as she scrutinized the numbers, Cass's face would flash in her mind, stubborn and resolute as she defended her team and their equipment. Evelyn grit her teeth, dismissing the vision as quickly as it came. It was just the residue of their last argument, she told herself. Nothing more. Yet, the impression lingered, her mind slipping back to the fire in Cass's eyes when they argued about those "outdated" tools and what she called "the spirit of the department."

Focus, she chided herself, shuffling the pages to block out thoughts of Cass. Efficiency was essential for sustainability; it was the only way forward for a department with limited funds and growing responsibilities. Every decision, no matter how unpopular, was ultimately for their benefit. Still, a shadow of doubt nagged at her.

The door swung open suddenly, and Evelyn looked up to find Cass filling the doorway. The captain's shoulders were tense, her gaze hard as it settled on Evelyn. A sheen of sweat covered her, and a faint coating of ash graced her face. She looked exhausted. Cass stepped inside, the door clicking shut behind her with a finality that made Evelyn's heart quicken.

"Still here?" Cass's tone was flat, edged with a coolness Evelyn recognized as frustration barely held in check.

"Yes," Evelyn replied, meeting Cass's gaze evenly. "I thought I'd go over the proposals one more time to make sure we're not overlooking any options. I'll be out of your hair now that you've returned" She kept her voice calm, measured, professional. Cass's jaw tensed, and Evelyn could feel the storm brewing beneath her steady exterior.

"Options," Cass repeated, crossing her arms. "Like cutting the equipment budget again?" Her voice was low, but the accusation cut through the room, heating the air between them.

Evelyn sighed, shifting her papers aside as she prepared herself for yet another clash. "We need to reallocate resources, Cass. I'm not doing this to undermine your team, but we have to operate within our means. This department is spending more than it's bringing in—"

Cass interrupted her, a spark igniting in her eyes. "It's not just numbers, Evelyn. Every dollar you cut is another risk we take. You're asking us to sacrifice safety for a budget projection." Her words were crisp, clipped, each one a verbal shove.

Evelyn's irritation flared, fueled by exhaustion and Cass's relentless pushback. She stood, crossing the room until they were nearly eye to eye. "I know what I'm asking for," she replied, her voice firmer. "But you don't seem to understand that if we don't start making these changes now, there might not be a department left to protect. This isn't about you or your team's pride; it's about the sustainability of the entire operation."

Cass's eyes flashed, and she took a step closer, her presence a wall of heat and determination. "Don't you dare question our commitment, Evelyn," she said, her tone low and dangerous. "We're out there every day, running into burning buildings while you sit behind a desk and count pennies."

The words struck a nerve, stinging in a way Evelyn hadn't expected. "I'm not questioning your commitment," she shot back, her voice rising with her anger. "But there's a difference between bravery and recklessness. New equipment could save lives, Cass, and if you'd stop being so damn stubborn, you'd see that."

Cass's blue eyes narrowed and some of her hair had escaped its tie, flying wild around her face, and Evelyn felt the tension ratchet up another degree, the air between them buzzing with a mix of frustration and something else—something almost magnetic. Cass took another step forward, close enough that Evelyn could feel the heat radiating from her, close enough that their eyes locked in an unbreakable line.

"Stubborn?" Cass echoed, her voice nearly a growl. "You don't know the first thing about what it means to lead this team. You think you can just waltz in here and start tearing down everything we've built without even understanding what it means to these people?"

"Maybe I understand more than you think," Evelyn replied, her own voice dropping, sharpened with irritation and a flicker of something she couldn't quite name. She held her ground, refusing to be intimidated by Cass's intensity. "You talk about loyalty and pride, but loyalty doesn't pay for the equipment you need, Cass. I'm trying to help, even if you don't want to see it."

Cass's hand clenched into a fist at her side, and Evelyn could feel the simmering anger radiating from her. The silence stretched between them, thick and heavy, and Evelyn's pulse raced in her throat. She was used to confrontations, used to people pushing back, but there was something different about this, something that felt personal, almost raw.

"You think this is helping?" Cass said, her voice low and tight. "All you're doing is stripping us down piece by piece, and you don't even care what it does to morale. To the people who rely on this department every single day."

Evelyn felt her own control start to slip, her frustration boiling over as she stepped even closer, their faces now inches apart. She could see the flecks of color of yellow and green in Cass's eyes, the stubborn set of her jaw, the faint tremor in her breathing. Her pulse raced, a thrill of defiance and something else—a thrill she tried to ignore but couldn't quite suppress.

"I care about this department just as much as you do, Cass," she said, her voice barely above a whisper. "But we're on borrowed time here. You can't cling to the past just because it feels safe."

Cass's hand shot out, grabbing her arm—not hard, but firm enough that Evelyn's breath hitched. The heat of Cass's touch seeped through her skin, igniting something electric that shot straight to her core. Evelyn's voice faltered, her heartbeat thundering in her ears as Cass's eyes bore into hers, searching, challenging.

"Safe?" Cass echoed, her voice rough, almost a whisper. "You think I don't know what's at stake? I live it every day, Evelyn. This isn't some spreadsheet for me. It's people. It's lives."

The intensity of her words hung in the air, charged and crackling. Evelyn couldn't look away, couldn't pull herself out of the magnetic pull between them. Cass's grip on her arm softened, but she didn't let go. Their faces were inches apart, their breaths mingling in the heated space, and Evelyn felt her own restraint slipping, the control she prided herself on dissolving in the face of Cass's raw passion.

Before she could think, before she could talk herself out of it, Evelyn leaned in, closing the gap between them. Cass's eyes widened, and for a brief second, Evelyn thought she'd misread the moment. But then Cass's hand slid up her arm, steadying her as her lips met Evelyn's, tentative at first, then deepening with a fervor that made Evelyn's knees weak.

The world fell away. The firehouse, the argument, the budget cuts—all of it dissolved in the heat of that kiss, a heady mix of frustration and something far more dangerous. Cass's mouth was warm and demanding, her grip firm and grounding, and Evelyn let herself fall into the sensation, her fingers tangling in the collar of Cass's shirt as she pulled her closer.

For a moment, they were lost, consumed by the passion that had been simmering between them, unacknowledged and unresolved. It was a release, a surrender, a crossing of lines they'd both been too stubborn to acknowledge until now. Evelyn's hands moved to Cass's shoulders, her grip desperate, as if anchoring herself in the intensity of the moment.

But just as suddenly, Cass pulled back, her breathing ragged as she looked at Evelyn, her eyes dark and unreadable. Evelyn's heart pounded, the weight of what they'd just done settling over her, but she couldn't bring herself to regret it.

Cass released her arm slowly, her gaze lingering on Evelyn's face, a mixture of frustration and something softer, something vulnerable. Evelyn opened her mouth to say something, to bridge the sudden silence, but no words came, and she realized with a jolt that she didn't know what to say.

Cass's voice was low, almost a whisper, as she finally spoke. "This...probably shouldn't have happened," she said, but there was no regret in her eyes, only a smoldering intensity that made Evelyn's pulse race all over again.

"Probably not," Evelyn replied, her voice soft, barely audible. But she didn't pull away, didn't move to leave.

Cass's limbs moved with a mind of their own, propelled by need, want. She pulled

Evelyn in closer, recapturing her soft lips with her own, firmer this time. She bit down, capturing Evelyn's lower lip between her teeth. She gripped the collar of Evelyn's perfectly crisp, white blouse in her rough fingers, pulling her into her roughly.

Evelyn didn't hesitate, giving in to the embrace in an instant, melting into Cass's strong arms. She wrapped her hands behind Cass's neck, tangling her fingers through the hair at her nape.

A final tug on Evelyn's lips, Cass pulled back, breath heaving. She held Evelyn's sharp chin in her fingers and locked eyes.

"We shouldn't be doing this."

"Probably not."

"Fuck it."

"I'd much rather you fucked me."

Cass chuckled. "Your wish is my command."

She moved even closer, turning her attention to Evelyn's neck, kissing and biting along its length, across her collar bone; all the while, she fought and tugged the buttons that ran down the front of Evelyn's blouse. Finally, she undid the last one, popping it through the loop. Cass tugged on the sleeves, watching as the fabric slid off Evelyn's shoulders, landing with a soft flumpf on the floor.

"Come here," Cass purred.

Evelyn strolled over casually, as though there was nothing the slightest bit out of the ordinary with their current circumstance.

"Turn around."

Cass leaned into her, pressing herself against Evelyn's back, running her hands up and over her shoulder and slinking down to her breasts. Evelyn felt herself shiver as Cass's calloused fingers dragged across her soft, sensitive skin. Cass slowly grazed her way down her stomach, around her hips, and up her spine, stopping to toy with her lacy bra strap.

"Is this what you want?" Cass whispered.

"God, yes."

Unhooking the strap, Cass let it fall to the floor, smiling. Cass's hands went to cup Evelyn's breasts and gently caress her nipples, and Evelyn let out a soft gasp. Cass plucked Evelyn's left nipple between two of her fingers, pulling gently, twisting only slightly.

Cass's hands dropped, and Evelyn let out a disappointed moan that quickly turned into impatience as Cass's fingers found their way to her belt, slowly sliding her pants down her hips.

She was still caught in her daydreams when Cass sauntered back to her, catching her off guard as she pushed Evelyn up against the office wall.

There was a gleam in Cass's eyes that Evelyn couldn't quite make out, and that spurred her on as she slipped out from beneath Cass's grasp and spun her around against the wall. "My turn now, don't you think, Captain?"

She pressed Cass's palms against the smooth, cold wall, hoping Cass got the message. No touching.

Cass's dark navy shirt was yanked from where it had been firmly tucked into her pants, and Evelyn began unbuttoning it. Precisely, methodically. Cass smirked as Evelyn undid the first three buttons, only to reveal a lighter blue shirt beneath.

"What idiot designed a uniform with two layers?" Evelyn muttered to herself.

She tugged at the hem of Cass's undershirt, pulling it loose. Moving the collar of the navy shirt to the side, she wrestled with the top several buttons before she grabbed at Cass's left arm.

"Up."

Cass obeyed, reaching both arms toward the ceiling as Evelyn pulled the pair of shirts up and over her head. Evelyn reached around and unclasped Cass's bra with practiced ease. Old and graying, the garment fell to the floor, starkly different to Evelyn's pretty black one that was strewn several feet away.

Evelyn stepped back, surveying Cass's topless form, still pressed against the wall.

"Like what you see?"

Evelyn didn't bother to reply. Instead, moving forward and ducking down, she took Cass's right nipple in her mouth.

Cass let out a keening moan as the hot wetness enveloped her. Evelyn began tonguing at the hardened nub—flicking it, circling it, biting ever so softly until Cass threw her head back in pleasure.

Evelyn's other hand teased over her left breast before sliding south, her long nails scraping over soft skin, to Cass's belt. Unbuckled, unbuttoned, unzipped. Her fingers crept past Cass's underwear and between her hot, slick folds. A pulse of need rippled through Evelyn as her fingers ghosted over Cass's clit.

"Fuck," Cass moaned.

"Shh, we wouldn't want anyone to hear you now, would we?"

Cass flashed her a half-hearted glare as she moved her hand from where it was to Evelyn's hip, sliding her hand down into the black lacy underwear. Cass slipped her rough fingers against her core and stroked in rhythm to match Evelyn's pace.

Every time Cass's fingers glided over her clit, she repaid in kind, each of them working faster and faster. Breathing hard. Skin on skin.

Evelyn couldn't hold it back any longer. Her climax building steadily, it wracked through her, shaking, trembling, her clit pulsing with want. Cass's hand stopped its motions, but Evelyn continued. Gradually firmer and faster until Cass, too, was shaking against her. Spent.

∽

As the adrenaline ebbed, Cass pulled back, her breathing still uneven as the weight of what they'd just done settled heavily between them. She looked at Evelyn, searching her face for something—maybe an answer to the vulnerability she suddenly felt. But Evelyn's expression had already shifted, her usual composed mask slipping back into place.

A silence hung in the air, thick and unresolved. Without a word, Evelyn recovered her clothes and gathered her things, her eyes flicking briefly over Cass before she turned and headed for the door. The quiet *click* of it closing felt like a final, unspoken line drawn between them.

~

In the hallway, Evelyn's steps echoed in the stillness of the firehouse. Her pulse raced, each beat a reminder of the undeniable connection she'd felt, but also of the thrill and alarm that lingered in its wake. She forced herself to focus, steeling her thoughts and telling herself it had been a lapse, nothing more. But as she walked out into the night, every detail of the moment in Cass's office replayed in her mind, leaving her rattled—and more than a little unsure of what might come next.

∽

Evelyn navigated the darkened streets of Phoenix Ridge, the steady rhythm of her tires against the pavement a stark contrast to the chaos in her mind. She forced herself to breathe, to compartmentalize the night and push it behind her. Yet despite her best efforts, she couldn't shake the lingering sense of excitement—and trouble—that Cass brought into her otherwise orderly world. The thrill of the unexpected burned in her chest, battling against the caution she'd built her career upon.

The road stretched out before Evelyn, dark and empty save for the rhythmic sweep of her headlights against the asphalt. The night air seeped in through the cracked window, cool against her flushed skin, but it did nothing to quiet the storm raging inside her. Her hands gripped the steering wheel tighter than necessary, the familiar tension in her jaw returning as she replayed the events of the evening in her mind.

What had she done? What had she *allowed* to happen? Her stomach twisted with a cocktail of guilt and frustration as she thought of Cass—of the way her resolve had crumbled the moment they were alone, of the fire in Cass's eyes that she'd been unable to resist. Giving in like that, letting herself be vulnerable…it was reckless, a mistake she couldn't afford to repeat.

The city lights flickered on the horizon as she drove, but Evelyn barely registered them. All she could focus on was the nagging voice in her head reminding her of everything she stood to lose. She'd worked so hard to build her career and earn her reputation as someone who could make the hard choices without letting emotions cloud her judgment. But tonight, she had let those emotions take control, and now she felt untethered, like a ship adrift in a storm.

Her chest tightened as she thought about Cass—not just the heat of their argument, the intensity of their connection, but the person beneath it all. Cass was everything Evelyn wasn't: passionate, grounded, unafraid to stand up for what she believed in. And that, Evelyn realized, was exactly the problem. Cass had a way of pulling her into a world she wasn't sure she belonged in, a world where emotions ran deep and logic wasn't always enough.

Evelyn sighed, her fingers drumming anxiously against the wheel as she stopped at a red light. The silence in the car was deafening, broken only by the soft hum of the engine. She had to regain control, to reassert the boundaries she'd let slip tonight. This wasn't just about her; it was about the job, the future of the department, and her responsibility to see this through. She couldn't let her feelings—whatever they were—derail everything she'd worked for.

When the light turned green, Evelyn pressed down on the gas, her determination hardening with every passing mile. By the time she reached her apartment, she had convinced herself that tonight would be a one-time lapse, a momentary weakness she wouldn't allow to happen again.

But as she climbed the stairs to her door and slipped inside, her resolve felt brittle, her mind still haunted by the memory of

Cass's touch, the fire in her voice, and the unspoken connection that had ignited between them. Evelyn shook her head, as if the action could rid her of the thoughts. She couldn't let this happen again. She wouldn't. Tomorrow, she told herself, she would focus. She would put everything back in its proper place.

She had to.

7

CASS

Cass couldn't shake the memory, no matter how hard she tried to bury it under the routines and responsibilities of her work. The firehouse had always been her anchor, a place where duty and purpose overrode everything else, where her focus never wavered. But ever since that night, Cass felt like she was fighting against an undertow, drawn toward thoughts of Evelyn against her will. The routine of each shift felt heavier now, her concentration slipping in moments she couldn't afford. A simple briefing with her team became an exercise in forcing herself to listen, to absorb the details, to drown out that flicker of something that lingered like an ember in her mind.

Evelyn. Her name felt like both a spark and a weight, something igniting inside Cass that she wasn't prepared to handle. Cass prided herself on her ability to separate personal feelings from work. She'd faced high-stakes situations, put herself in danger for her team, and yet this—whatever this was—was testing her like nothing ever had.

But it wasn't just Evelyn's presence or even her sharp eyes or biting words. It was what Evelyn stood for: the challenges, the constant friction, and the unyielding strength in her gaze. It drove Cass crazy, the way Evelyn pushed back at every turn. It infuriated her, this woman who'd come in with her cost-cutting plans and her steady, relentless focus on efficiency. But beneath the frustration simmered something more dangerous, something that stirred in Cass a craving she didn't want to admit.

She spent the days after their encounter trying to rationalize her behavior, trying to understand why she'd let herself slip. She knew how much the firehouse meant to her; she'd dedicated years to this job, to her team,

Playing with Fire

and now, by allowing herself to be distracted by Evelyn, she felt she was letting them down. She imagined Becky's voice in her head—the wise, encouraging words of her mentor, now a legend in Phoenix Ridge but someone who'd trusted her to lead. Cass couldn't help but feel that she'd broken that trust somehow, that she'd let her guard down and lost sight of what was important. And that mistake was weighing on her, pressing down on her chest with each thought of Evelyn.

The rest of the week passed in a haze, each hour filled with drills, inspections, and meetings—all attempts to bury herself in her work. She wanted to stay too busy to think, too busy to let herself drift back into the memory of Evelyn's eyes meeting hers, of the electric pull that had surged between them. Yet no matter how hard she tried, Evelyn lingered in her thoughts, frustratingly persistent. It was as if each thought, each memory of that night only strengthened the need to confront her and make sense of what had happened.

By Friday, Cass felt stretched thin, her focus shattered by the constant back-and-forth in her mind. She tried avoiding Evelyn and keeping her distance, hoping that time would blunt the intensity of her feelings. But instead, avoiding Evelyn only intensified her frustration, her thoughts spiraling into restless confusion every time she remembered the spark in Evelyn's gaze, the unspoken challenge they both seemed to feel.

Late one evening, unable to sleep, Cass reached for her phone. She scrolled through her contacts until she found Evelyn's name. Her thumb hovered over the call button, but she couldn't bring herself to press it. Instead, she tossed her phone aside, a fresh wave of frustration welling up within her. She didn't understand this pull toward Evelyn; it was reckless and went against everything she stood for. But the need to resolve things, to confront what had happened, was growing louder, harder to ignore.

Finally, as if compelled by some force outside her control, Cass found herself driving to Evelyn's office.

Cass gripped the steering wheel, her knuckles pale against the worn leather as she drove through the quiet streets toward Evelyn's office. She'd told herself over and over that she'd gotten a handle on her feelings, that she could compartmentalize them like everything else in her life. But as she replayed their last tense exchange in her mind, she felt the same pull—an ache of unresolved tension, of words left unsaid, and of emotions she couldn't shake no matter how hard she tried. Every rational part of her had advised against this, warned her that driving over to see Evelyn now, at night, was a dangerous game. Yet here she was, unable to stop herself.

She glanced at the clock on the dashboard, the late hour reminding her that Evelyn would be alone, likely absorbed in her work. That image sent a thrill through her, a quiet sense of anticipation that she'd been trying to ignore since they'd first collided, both literally and figuratively, over their duties and loyalties. This wasn't like her; Cass had always prided herself on keeping control, on separating her personal life from her responsibilities. But something about Evelyn—her resilience, her defiance, the way she stood toe-to-toe with Cass without backing down—had unraveled her usual resolve, leaving her vulnerable to an impulse she couldn't quite explain.

Cass shook her head, trying to quiet the doubts, but the tension only grew with each passing mile. She knew this was more than a work conflict now; it was something she hadn't felt in years, a pull that was equal parts desire and challenge. The thought of confronting Evelyn, of finally speaking openly—of doing something reckless—both terrified and exhilarated her. As the office building came into view, Cass felt her pulse quicken, her grip on the wheel tightening as she parked. She knew whatever happened tonight would change things between them, and yet, despite the uncertainty, she couldn't bring herself to turn back.

It was late, the building was dimly lit, and Cass's footsteps echoed in the empty hallways. She didn't know exactly what she was planning to say, but she needed answers, needed to face this thing between them head-on.

Cass arrived at Evelyn's office after-hours, her heart pounding in her chest as she made her way through the dimly lit hallways. The building was nearly empty, giving her surroundings an eerie, hushed quality that only heightened her tension. She didn't know exactly what she wanted to say to Evelyn, but she knew she needed answers—needed to understand why she couldn't let this go.

When she entered, Evelyn was there, alone at her desk, a stack of papers spread out before her. She looked up, a flicker of surprise passing over her face as she saw Cass standing in the doorway. But she quickly masked it, her gaze shifting to that unreadable, professional demeanor Cass was beginning to know all too well.

"Cass," Evelyn said, her voice even, though Cass sensed a subtle wariness beneath her calm tone. "I wasn't expecting you."

Cass took a steadying breath, walking further into the office, her gaze locked on Evelyn's. The tension in the room was like a live wire, the space seeming to shrink as she stepped closer. She could feel her heartbeat thudding in her chest, a blend of anger, frustration, and something else she didn't dare name.

"I wanted to talk about...what happened," Cass began, her voice rough and low, betraying the emotions she'd tried so hard to suppress.

Evelyn's expression softened, just a fraction, her eyes meeting Cass's with an intensity that sent a shiver down her spine. "Is that so?" Evelyn's voice was controlled, but Cass could sense the vulnerability lurking beneath her professional mask, a hint of something she didn't expect.

Cass clenched her fists, trying to ground herself, to push back the emotions threatening to boil over. "That wasn't supposed to happen," she said, her voice thick with a mixture of anger and regret. "I don't... I don't cross lines like that. I don't know what's gotten into me."

For a brief moment, Evelyn's gaze softened further, and Cass saw a glimmer of understanding in her eyes, a flicker of vulnerability that made her heart twist. "Maybe it wasn't supposed to happen," Evelyn replied, her voice quieter now, almost tender. "But it did."

Evelyn's words, the honesty in them, broke through Cass's defenses, igniting the frustration and desire she'd been holding back. She stepped closer, the air between them thick and charged, her pulse racing as Evelyn's gaze held steady, unwavering. Cass could feel the magnetic pull drawing her in, stronger than the restraint she'd clung to all week.

"Evelyn..." Cass's voice was barely a whisper, a mix of anger and longing, a plea wrapped in a warning.

Evelyn straightened, her eyes never leaving Cass's. "What are you really here for, Cass?"

The question cut through her defenses, a question she didn't want to answer. She didn't have words for the storm raging inside her, the turmoil of desire and frustration.

Without thinking, Cass reached out, her hand brushing against Evelyn's arm. She felt the tension in Evelyn's muscles, the barely contained energy beneath the surface. Evelyn's gaze met hers, sharp and unwavering, and in that moment, the air between them shifted, the weight of their unspoken feelings pressing in on them, undeniable and electric.

The words hung in the air between them, weighty and raw, stirring up every emotion Cass had been trying to ignore. It was like holding back a flood, the force of it pushing and pulling until finally, something broke. Without another thought, Cass stepped forward, closing the last inches between them in a single, heated motion. Her hands found Evelyn's face, and she pulled her into a kiss that was fierce, unrestrained—a release of all the frustration, desire, and unspoken feelings that had been building for so long.

The instant her lips met Evelyn's, a rush of heat flooded through Cass, coursing from her head to her fingertips. It was unlike anything she'd felt before—intense, consuming, and completely beyond her control. She felt like she was falling and grounding herself all at once, each touch, each movement fanning the flames that had been smoldering between them for weeks. There was nothing gentle about it; it was raw, an expression of everything she'd held back, the kind of kiss that felt more like a collision than an embrace. Evelyn's hands slid up her arms, gripping her shoulders as if she needed to steady herself, the touch sending another shock through Cass's system.

As they broke apart just enough to catch their breath, Cass didn't hesitate. She felt an unshakable need to hold her closer, to deepen the connection she'd been denying herself. In one smooth motion, her hands slid to Evelyn's waist, lifting her effortlessly as if she weighed nothing. Evelyn's breath hitched, her eyes widening in surprise for just a second before softening as Cass set her down on the edge of the desk, never breaking eye contact. Cass could see the spark in Evelyn's eyes, the vulnerability and excitement mirroring her own.

She felt a surge of confidence, her usual steadfastness merging with the reckless thrill of finally letting go, of surrendering to this pull between them. Her mind was spinning —torn between wanting to say something and ground herself in words, but knowing that no words would capture the depth of what she was feeling.

The doubt and conflict she'd carried around vanished, replaced with the clarity of this moment. Cass felt herself letting down every wall, every reservation and her thoughts of the department, her team, and her responsibilities fading into the background as she gave in. For once, there was nothing but the two of them, the undeniable magnetism drawing her to Evelyn, the realization that she'd wanted this—wanted *her*—far more than she'd ever let herself believe.

Her hands gripped the edge of the desk as she leaned in, lips brushing along Evelyn's in a gentler, more searching kiss, but her pulse continued to race, every part of her alive with the sheer intensity of being this close.

She moved away, kissing softly as she went. Down her neck, her chest, stomach, and her thighs over the neatly ironed skirt Evelyn was wearing today. Down each leg, kissing the soft stocking material that, although sheer, hid the Evelyn's skin from Cass's gaze.

Down and down she went, until finally reaching her feet, encased in shiny black heels, whose clicking had become the background music to Cass's every thought, awake and in dreams. She ran her finger along the toe of the shoe, taking in the smooth, unscuffed surface, so very different to her own worn-in work boots. God, they really did come from such different worlds. But right now that didn't matter. What mattered was the woman in front of her. She wanted to have her. Touch her. Taste her.

Slowly, teasingly, she slid her hands up Evelyn's legs, tracing circles with her thumbs all the way up her inner thighs, not breaking eye contact for even a second. She could see the glint of anticipation in Evelyn's eyes, the flush on her cheeks; she was breathing shallowly, her eyes glazed over with want.

"Mmm, I wonder what you would do if I just tore these stockings right open to get to your pussy? How you would feel driving home all disheveled." She grinned as Evelyn's eyes snapped to hers, a shocked expression on her face. "It was only a thought; I'm sure I couldn't afford to replace them anyway."

Her hands continued their journey upwards, Evelyn letting out a mewl as Cass hiked up her skirt to her hips. There, beneath the stockings, Cass could make out her panties. Red. Lace again, but red. How naughty. Cass would bet her month's paycheck that her bra matched, but she didn't want to distract from her goal to find out.

Fingering the waistband of the stockings and underwear, she tugged them down.

Evelyn tilted her hips, needing no encouragement; she wanted them off as badly as Cass did. Sweeping both Evelyn's legs in a smooth motion, Cass tossed them over her shoulder, hearing them land softly behind her.

Finally, Evelyn was bare to Cass's gaze, completely shaved and smooth, just a hint of darker pink peeking through.

"Now, don't be too loud. Can't have any of your big, powerful bosses knowing what you get up to in your office." Cass smirked as she dropped to her knees, kissing and teasing her way up the soft skin of Evelyn's thighs, until she reached her prize.

She didn't hesitate, diving in to claim Evelyn's pretty pussy in her mouth. Her tongue found the clit quickly, flicking across it back and forth before drawing away. Cass had no desire for Evelyn to finish any time soon. She wanted to draw it out, drive the woman wild with need, to watch her unravel, all because of Cass.

She drew wide, languid circles with her tongue, lapping it over and over softly. After a while, she sucked, ever so slightly, and Evelyn's hands shot down to tangle themselves in Cass's short hair in response.

Then back to the circles, slow and soft. Over and over, Cass teased her, switching back and forth. Bringing her closer to the edge before backing away.

Cass's jaw was beginning to ache, and she could feel Evelyn shaking above her, desperate to climax. Once again, she drew circles, concentrating more firmly on Evelyn's clit. When she could sense that she was near her breaking point, Cass brought her fingers up, slipping them into Evelyn's core, pumping them back and forth as she licked and sucked. Closer and closer, until finally, Evelyn jolted above her, tremors racing their way through her whole body. Only once Evelyn's climax had finished did Cass pull back, her knees complaining. Fuck, Evelyn looked practically debauched up there. Her hair was a mess, her clothes crumpled, her cheeks flushed, and her body thoroughly worn out, Cass thought Evelyn had never looked better.

The engine's low hum filled the cab of Cass's truck as she drove through the quiet streets, the streetlights casting fleeting shadows across her face. She gripped the steering wheel tightly, her knuckles white against the dark leather, as if holding on a little harder could anchor her to some semblance of stability. But no amount of tension in her hands could distract her from the swirling chaos in her head.

She had done it again. Let herself lose control, give in to something she didn't fully understand. The memory of Evelyn's touch, the heat of her breath, the undeniable pull that had drawn them together burned in her mind, refusing to fade.

"What the hell am I doing?" Cass muttered, her voice harsh in the enclosed space.

She glanced at the rearview mirror as though searching for answers in her own reflection, but all she saw was a face lined with frustration and something she couldn't quite name. She felt like a stranger to herself tonight, torn between conflicting emotions that refused to settle.

Anger bubbled up in her chest, hot and sharp. She wasn't even sure who it was aimed at—Evelyn, for getting under her skin in ways no one else ever had; herself, for letting it happen; or the situation they were in, with its impossible tangle of professional boundaries and undeniable chemistry.

Cass smacked the steering wheel with the heel of her hand, the sharp sound breaking through the oppressive silence. "Get it together," she growled, her voice cutting through the haze of her thoughts.

But she couldn't get it together. Not when every mile she drove felt like she was getting further from the office but closer to a chasm she didn't know how to cross. How could she let this happen? She was a professional, a leader. She had spent years keeping her personal life separate from her work, ensuring nothing ever interfered with her responsibilities to the firehouse and her team.

And yet, Evelyn Ford had come into her life like a spark in dry brushwood, igniting something Cass hadn't even realized was there.

Her jaw clenched as she replayed the night in her mind, every moment etched into her memory with a clarity that felt almost cruel. She hated how easily Evelyn had unraveled her, how the fiery arguments and charged silences had turned into something else entirely. Evelyn, with her sharp wit and unreadable eyes, her unshakable determination and that damn infuriating way of always meeting Cass head-on, refusing to back down.

And now Cass couldn't stop thinking about her. It was maddening.

She glanced at the clock on the dashboard. It was late, far too late to still be wrestling with this. Her team was counting on her. They were fighting a battle for their future, for the tools and resources they needed to save lives, and Cass couldn't afford to let herself get distracted. She'd always prided herself on being unshakable, on putting her duty first. But now? Now, she felt like she was coming apart at the seams.

Her thoughts drifted, unbidden, back to Evelyn's expression as they had parted. There had been something in her eyes—something vulnerable, almost hesitant that Cass hadn't been able to ignore. It had made her heart ache in a way she didn't want to examine too closely.

"Damn it," Cass muttered, shaking her

head as if the motion could dislodge the memory.

Her anger swelled again, mixing with frustration and confusion until it was a storm raging inside her. She wanted to blame Evelyn, to pin all of this on her. But deep down, Cass knew better. This wasn't something Evelyn had done to her. It was something they had both let happen, something that felt as inevitable as it was dangerous.

By the time Cass pulled into her driveway, her mind was no clearer than it had been when she had left Evelyn's office. She turned off the engine and sat in the darkness, her hands still gripping the wheel. She needed to figure out how to handle this—how to untangle the mess of emotions and focus on what really mattered.

But as she leaned her head back against the seat, Evelyn's face flickered in her mind once more, and Cass knew it wasn't going to be that simple.

8

EVELYN

Evelyn sat in her office, staring at her laptop, the usual flurry of budget reports and efficiency projections fading into an uncharacteristic blur. For the first time in as long as she could remember, her thoughts refused to obey the discipline she'd always prided herself on. Her work was her armor, her way of maintaining control in a world that often demanded more from her than she could give. But now, despite her best efforts, her mind kept returning to Cass Harris—the fierce, stubborn, infuriating fire captain who seemed determined to throw Evelyn's world into chaos.

It wasn't just the arguments, though

those alone were maddening. Every interaction with Cass seemed to chip away at Evelyn's carefully constructed defenses, the ones she'd perfected over years of working in environments where authority and respect were hard-won. Cass challenged her in a way no one else had. And instead of driving her away, that fire in Cass, that fierce loyalty and unshakable determination, pulled her in closer. Each time they clashed, each time Cass's sharp words cut through Evelyn's carefully measured logic, she felt something inside her shift, unsettling her in ways she couldn't explain.

For days, Cass and Evelyn had been at each other's throats over every conceivable issue, their once-professional interactions now laced with sharp barbs and simmering frustration. It started with budget cuts—her relentless push to streamline the department clashing with Cass's fierce defense of her team's morale. Then it spiraled into debates over equipment upgrades, training methods, and even small operational decisions like response times and shift schedules. Each disagreement felt more personal than the last, their voices rising over everything from staffing needs to safety protocols. Every interaction had become a battleground, with Cass accusing Evelyn of being out of touch with the realities on the ground, while Evelyn snapped back that Cass was too sentimental and too emotionally attached to traditions. The tension between them was palpable, thickening the air in every room they entered, making it impossible to ignore the crackling energy that neither of them seemed able—or willing—to resolve.

Evelyn took a steadying breath, her hand hovering over the keyboard as she tried to will herself back to her work. But memories of that night and the kiss they'd shared slipped into her mind unbidden. She felt her cheeks warm, a thrill that was equal parts frustration and undeniable attraction rushing through her. How had she let it get this far? She had always been able to compartmentalize her feelings, to prioritize her work above all else. She'd never been one to mix business with anything personal. Yet here she was, haunted by the memory of Cass's hands and mouth on her, her fierce, challenging gaze softened just enough to show Evelyn a glimpse of something deeper.

The days passed, each one bringing new attempts to rebuild the distance she knew she needed to keep. She spent hours at her desk, late nights and early mornings poring over reports and formulating plans for the department. But no matter how many times she reminded herself of her mission, her purpose for being here, her thoughts inevitably circled back to Cass. There was an undeniable intensity in Cass that Evelyn had never encountered, a raw passion that stirred something in her she'd long since buried.

That passion resurfaced during their next meeting at the station. Evelyn's resolve faltered as she entered the firehouse, her gaze sweeping over the familiar surroundings that now felt different, charged with a tension she couldn't ignore. She spotted Cass across the room, talking to a group of her team members, her presence as commanding as ever. When their eyes met, Evelyn felt that familiar jolt—a quickening of her pulse, a flare of something deep within her.

"Captain Harris," she greeted, her voice

clipped, attempting to keep things strictly professional. But Cass's eyes held hers, and Evelyn's façade began to crack.

"Evelyn." Cass's tone was calm, but there was a challenge in her eyes, one that made Evelyn's carefully constructed walls tremble. Cass crossed her arms, her eyes narrowing as she stared at Evelyn. "You really think slashing our budget is the answer?" she snapped. "You don't even understand the day-to-day operations. These changes aren't going to improve anything; they're just going to tear us apart."

Evelyn stood her ground, her back straight, the steel in her posture betraying none of the discomfort she felt inside. "I'm looking at the bigger picture, Cass. The department's future depends on adaptation. You can't keep clinging to the way things have always been." She lifted her chin, the words coming out sharper than she intended. "Efficiency doesn't mean we lose heart. It means we're prepared for what's coming."

Cass took a step closer, her gaze intense. "You're not hearing me. You think you can just impose your way without understanding what we're up against, what we've built here. People aren't numbers, Evelyn. You're losing sight of that."

The air between them crackled, the words fading in comparison to the tension humming beneath the surface. Evelyn's chest tightened as she met Cass's gaze, and for a moment, the argument didn't seem to matter anymore. The heat between them—unspoken, simmering—was undeniable. She opened her mouth to respond, but the words stuck in her throat. Instead, she found herself fixated on the way Cass's jaw clenched, how her lips parted as if ready to say something else, something that wasn't just about policy.

Cass's frustration flared, her voice growing louder with each word. "We've been having this same argument for days, Evelyn! Over and over again. You're not listening. You're just pushing your plan without even considering the consequences. You're bulldozing through, and it's like you don't even care about the people who actually have to carry this out." She threw her hands up, exasperated. "This isn't about policy for us; it's about real lives, real work."

Evelyn's eyes flashed with a mix of irritation and something else, something sharper. "I'm listening, Cass. But the fact is, we don't have time for endless discussion. The department needs change, and I'm trying to make sure we have a future. If we don't cut costs now, there won't be a team to lead." Her voice was colder now, more controlled, as though the emotional undercurrent between them wasn't even there. "You think this is easy for me?" Cass shot back. "I don't want to see our team struggle. But your way—this cold, calculated approach—it won't work. We need to adapt, yes, but we also need to respect what we've built. I won't just let you tear it all down because you don't understand the stakes."

Evelyn shook her head, her voice steady but tired. "We're going around in circles, Cass. You don't trust my vision, and I don't trust your resistance to change. We're not getting anywhere with this." Her tone softened, just slightly, as she took a step back. "But the longer we argue, the more it feels like we're both fighting something...that isn't about this department anymore." She caught herself, realizing the weight of her words as soon as they left her mouth.

The shift in their dynamic was undeniable. The words they'd been saying no longer seemed to matter as much as the space between them. The tension that had been building for days now felt like it might explode.

Cass took a deep breath, her fingers curling at her sides. "We've been doing this dance for too long," she said, her voice rough with a mix of anger and something softer. "I just don't know what you want from me anymore."

Evelyn's eyes softened for a split second, a flicker of something unguarded. "I don't know either," she admitted quietly, her voice barely above a whisper. "But whatever this is, it's not helping either of us."

At a lull in their argument, Evelyn found herself faltering, her frustration mounting alongside her growing attraction. Her voice softened, and the usual coolness in her tone faded. "This is...difficult for me," she admitted, her words tumbling out before she could stop herself. She saw Cass's expression soften in response, a spark of understanding in her eyes that made Evelyn's heart clench.

"Why?" Cass asked, her voice low, as though sensing the vulnerability in Evelyn's admission.

Evelyn hesitated, the weight of her emotions pressing down on her. "Because I'm supposed to be here to do a job. I've done this so many times before. I walk in, make the changes that need to be made, and I leave. It's clean, efficient. But this time..." She searched for the right words to convey what she felt.. "You, this place, it's different."

Cass stepped closer, and Evelyn's pulse quickened, her heartbeat thrumming in her ears. "Maybe it's time to let down some of those walls," Cass said, her voice barely above a whisper, the intensity in her gaze pulling Evelyn in, grounding her in a way she hadn't expected.

Evelyn swallowed, her carefully guarded control slipping further as she held Cass's gaze. "I don't know how," she murmured. There was a rawness in her voice, a vulnerability she hadn't allowed herself to feel in years.

Cass's eyes softened, and without thinking, Evelyn reached for her, her hand resting on Cass's arm as she allowed herself to feel, to let go of the constant need for control. Cass's hand covered hers, warm and reassuring, and in that moment, Evelyn felt a strange sense of calm, a feeling she hadn't even realized she was missing.

They stood in silence, the charged air between them thickening as Evelyn's defenses crumbled. And then, as if drawn by an invisible force, Cass leaned in, her hand brushing against Evelyn's cheek. The tenderness in her touch was unexpected, sending a shiver down Evelyn's spine as she closed the gap between them.

Their kiss was softer this time, more tentative, yet filled with an intensity that spoke of the barriers they'd both fought so hard to maintain. Evelyn felt herself melting into Cass, the tension and frustration that had built between them dissolving in that moment of shared vulnerability.

When they pulled apart, Evelyn felt a flicker of uncertainty, her usual self-assuredness replaced by a quiet thrill that left her feeling exposed yet alive. Cass's hand lingered on her arm, grounding her, anchoring her in the present as they stood together in the dim light of the firehouse.

Neither of them spoke as Cass led her to the captain's office.

Cass stood close to Evelyn, the space between them charged but tender, her pulse thrumming in her ears. Evelyn's fingers hovered near the hem of Cass's shirt, a question lingering in her soft, searching eyes. Cass nodded, her breath catching as Evelyn's touch brushed her skin. Slowly, Evelyn lifted the fabric, her movements deliberate, as if every second mattered. The shirt slid off, pooling in Cass's hand before she let it drop to the floor.

Cass returned the gesture, her hands trembling slightly as they found the buttons of Evelyn's blouse. One by one, the tension between them unraveled, each button revealing more of the woman beneath. Evelyn let the blouse slip off her shoulders, and Cass swallowed hard, overwhelmed by the quiet vulnerability in Evelyn's expression.

They moved closer, skin brushing skin, their breaths mingling in the stillness. Cass wrapped her arms around Evelyn's waist, pulling her into a gentle embrace. Their bodies fit together as if they'd always belonged, and Cass closed her eyes, savoring the warmth. Evelyn's fingers traced along Cass's back, hesitant at first but growing surer with each pass, as if memorizing the feel of her.

For the first time, the walls between them felt miles away.

There was no raw urgency to them this time. No fiery passion, just gentle longing touches as they gave in to the tension that had engulfed them since their first meeting.

Cass ran her hand along Evelyn's shoulder, brushing her hair behind, and Evelyn shivered at her touch. Gently tugging her hand, she pulled Evelyn down onto the pullout bed. It creaked slightly under their shared weight, and they both held their breath, waiting for some noise outside to indicate that someone had heard.

Silence.

Cass took her time kissing and touching Evelyn, making her way up and down her body, paying attention to anywhere that elicited a gasp or soft moan. Evelyn responded, playing with Cass's breasts. Squeezing, tugging. Fuck, it felt amazing. As

Evelyn continued, Cass worked her way down to Evelyn's pussy, finding it already slick and hot.

Sucking and licking on her breasts, Cass slipped two fingers between her folds, slowly pumping back and forth. The sensations washed over Evelyn, her core curling tighter and tighter with each stroke. Her finish flooded through her quickly, throbbing and pulsing. She let it subside before looking at Cass, still situated between her legs, a pleased smirk across her face.

Evelyn dropped to her knees as Cass leant back against the wall. Evelyn buried her face between Cass's legs, her hungry mouth going straight to work on Cass's pussy. Her tongue delving and lapping and sucking.

Cass's deep guttural moans were driving her absolutely crazy.

It wasn't long until Cass's own climax wracked through her as Evelyn flicked her tongue back and forth over her clit, Cass bucking up into her mouth wildly, fighting to keep her moans silent. The energy that had filled them faded, replaced by a contented, sleepy haze.

Evelyn lay still, her head resting on Cass's shoulder, the pullout bed beneath them creaking faintly as their combined weight shifted. The room was silent, save for the rhythmic hum of the firehouse in the distance—the muffled buzz of voices, the faint thrum of the building's heating system, the occasional crackle of a radio. It was a stillness Evelyn wasn't accustomed to, one that made her hyperaware of the warmth of Cass's arm around her, the steady rise and fall of her chest, and the faint scent of soap lingering on her skin.

It should have been unsettling, lying here in the arms of someone who, only days ago, had felt like her most vocal adversary. But instead, it felt strangely right—natural, even. Cass held her with a certainty that Evelyn wasn't sure she'd ever experienced before, as if her presence here, in this moment, wasn't just accepted but essential.

That thought should have terrified her. It *did* terrify her.

Evelyn closed her eyes, willing her racing thoughts to quiet. Her entire career had been built on discipline and detachment, on making the tough calls and keeping emotions at arm's length. She'd spent years learning to shield herself from vulnerability, to focus on the goals and objectives at hand without letting personal entanglements muddy the waters. And yet, here she was—wrapped in the arms of a woman who had challenged her at every turn, who had infuriated her more than anyone else ever had, and who now had the power to completely unravel her.

She hadn't planned for this. She hadn't wanted this.

And yet...

Evelyn shifted slightly, her hand brushing against Cass's, their fingers tangling instinctively. The contact sent a faint shiver down her spine, and she cursed herself for how easily her body responded to Cass's touch. She was supposed to be the one in control, the one who kept her emotions neatly compartmentalized. But Cass...Cass had obliterated all of that with a single look, a single touch, a single whispered word.

How did I let this happen?

It wasn't just the physical pull, though

that was undeniable. It was the way Cass looked at her, as if she could see through every carefully constructed wall Evelyn had built over the years. It was the fire in her eyes when they argued, the passion that blazed so fiercely it left Evelyn both awed and unnerved. Cass had a way of making her feel exposed, vulnerable in a way she hadn't allowed herself to be in years. And yet, Evelyn couldn't bring herself to pull away.

She opened her eyes again, staring at the ceiling as she let herself feel the weight of Cass's arm across her stomach, the steady warmth of her body against hers. This wasn't supposed to be possible. Evelyn had spent so much time convincing herself that her job left no room for distractions like this, that she couldn't afford to let anyone in—not when she had a role to play, not when she had a reputation to uphold.

But Cass didn't feel like a distraction. She felt like gravity, like an irresistible force that Evelyn couldn't fight even if she wanted to.

Her mind drifted back to the arguments they'd had over the past few weeks, the tension that had built with every confrontation. At the time, Evelyn had told herself it was just professional friction, the inevitable clash of two strong-willed people with opposing views. But now, lying here in the quiet of the firehouse, she couldn't deny that it had always been more than that.

Cass had gotten under her skin from the moment they met. She'd seen through Evelyn's polished façade, challenged her in ways no one else ever had. And somewhere along the way, Evelyn had stopped dreading their arguments and started craving them, started looking forward to the way Cass's eyes would flash with determination, the way her voice would carry that fiery edge that made Evelyn's pulse quicken.

And now...now they were here, tangled together in a way that felt as inevitable as it was terrifying.

Evelyn's fingers tightened slightly around Cass's, and she felt the faintest pressure in return—a silent reassurance that made her chest ache in a way she didn't quite understand. She turned her head slightly, her gaze flickering to Cass's face. Her features were softer now, her expression unguarded in a way Evelyn rarely saw. The lines of tension that so often creased her brow were gone, replaced by a quiet peace that made Evelyn's heart clench.

She's beautiful, Evelyn thought, the admission startling in its simplicity. It wasn't just the physical—though Cass's sharp cheekbones and piercing blue eyes were impossible to ignore—it was the strength and vulnerability she carried in equal measure, the way she fought for what she believed in with an intensity that was both maddening and inspiring.

Evelyn let out a quiet sigh, her breath catching slightly as she felt Cass shift beside her, her arm tightening just enough to pull Evelyn closer. The gesture was so natural that it sent a pang of longing through Evelyn's chest. She wanted to stay here, to let herself sink into the warmth and safety of Cass's embrace, to forget about the job and the cuts and all the reasons this could never work.

But she couldn't.

The thought hit her like a bucket of cold water, and she swallowed hard, her chest tightening as reality came rushing back. This —whatever this was—couldn't last. She'd let herself get swept up in the moment, let herself give in to feelings she couldn't afford to have. But tomorrow, when the sun rose and the firehouse came back to life, they would still be on opposite sides of this fight.

And Evelyn would have to choose.

She would have to decide whether to let herself fall deeper into this connection with Cass, knowing it could jeopardize everything she'd worked for, or to pull away, to put up the walls again and focus on the job she'd come here to do.

It wasn't a choice she wanted to make. But it was a choice she'd have to make.

For now, though, she let herself stay. Just a little longer. Just until the pull of Cass's warmth and the quiet steadiness of her breathing lulled her into a dream-filled sleep.

9

CASS

Cass woke slowly, her senses pulling her from sleep in fragments. The muted morning light seeped through the cracks in her blinds, brushing against her closed eyelids. Her bed felt warmer than usual, and there was the faintest scent of lavender in the air. For a few blissful moments, she lingered in that twilight between dreams and reality, her body heavy with contentment. Then she felt the soft weight of an arm draped over her waist, and everything came rushing back.

Her eyes snapped open, and she turned her head slightly. There, lying peacefully beside her on the narrow pullout bed, was Evelyn. Her blonde hair was tousled against the pillow, her face relaxed in sleep. The vulnerability of that moment caught Cass off guard. Evelyn, who was always so composed and unreadable, looked entirely different now—soft, almost fragile. Cass's chest tightened, a swirl of emotions she couldn't quite name making her stomach churn.

For a moment, she simply lay there, listening to the quiet rhythm of Evelyn's breathing. The memory of the previous night played in her mind, vivid and inescapable. The way their tension had finally snapped, giving way to something raw and undeniable. The heat of their connection, the intensity of every touch—it was like nothing Cass had ever experienced before.

But now, in the cold light of morning, reality pressed down on her like a weight. They were still on opposite sides of a professional battlefield, still fighting for entirely different visions of the department's future. Nothing about their situation had changed, except now they'd crossed a line that couldn't be uncrossed.

Cass shifted slightly, careful not to wake Evelyn as she slipped out of bed. She ran a hand through her hair, frustration prickling at her nerves. What the hell was she doing? What *were* they doing?

She grabbed her clothes from where they'd been hastily discarded and dressed quietly, her movements stiff with unease. Glancing back at the bed, she saw Evelyn stir, her eyes fluttering open. For a brief moment, their gazes met, and Cass saw a flicker of something in Evelyn's expression—uncertainty, perhaps, or maybe regret. But then Evelyn's lips curled into a faint smile, and the tension between them seemed to shift again, like a pendulum swinging back and forth.

"Good morning," Evelyn said softly, her voice husky from sleep.

"Morning," Cass replied, her tone more gruff than she intended. She sat on the edge of the bed, rubbing the back of her neck. "You, uh...sleep okay?"

Evelyn chuckled lightly, sitting up and wrapping the sheet around herself. "Considering this bed is barely big enough for one person? Surprisingly well."

Cass smirked despite herself but quickly sobered. "Look, Evelyn..." Her voice trailed off as she searched for the right words. "About last night, I don't know what to say."

Evelyn tilted her head, her expression unreadable again. "You don't have to say anything, Cass. It happened. We can't change that."

Cass nodded, but the knot in her chest only tightened. "Yeah, but we can't just...ignore it either. This complicates everything."

"Complicated seems to be our default setting," Evelyn replied, a hint of wry humor in her tone. But there was a flicker of something deeper in her eyes, a vulnerability that mirrored Cass's own.

Before Cass could respond, her phone buzzed on the desk across the room. She grabbed it, grateful for the distraction, and saw Becky Thompson's name on the screen.

"I need to take this," she said, glancing at Evelyn.

Evelyn nodded, her expression guarded. "Of course."

Cass stepped outside, the cool morning air hitting her skin like a wake-up call. She answered the call, and Becky's warm, familiar voice greeted her from across the world.

"Morning, kid. Or I guess it's evening there, huh?"

Cass exhaled, the sound carrying all the tension she'd been holding. "Hey, Chief. Yeah, it's morning. How's Italy?"

"Beautiful as always," Becky said with a chuckle. "But I'm guessing you didn't answer just to hear about my pasta and wine adventures. What's on your mind?"

Cass hesitated, her fingers tapping against the phone. "It's...complicated."

"Everything worth doing usually is. Spill it."

Cass sighed, leaning against the wall. "It's Evelyn. The consultant."

"The one trying to gut your budget?" Becky's tone sharpened.

"Yeah. But it's not just that anymore." She paused, the words heavy in her throat. "We've...gotten close. Too close."

There was a beat of silence on the other end of the line before Becky spoke, her voice gentler now. "How close are we talking?"

"Last night kind of close."

Becky let out a low whistle. "Well, damn. Didn't see that coming."

"Neither did I," Cass admitted. "And now,

I don't know what to do. It's like every time we're in the same room, I can't think straight. But she's still pushing for changes that could hurt my team, Becky. I can't let that happen."

Becky was quiet for a moment, and when she spoke again, her tone was thoughtful. "Cass, you're one of the most grounded people I know. If this is throwing you off that much, it's worth paying attention to. But you're right—you can't let it interfere with your job. You've got a responsibility to your people."

"I know," Cass said, her voice barely above a whisper. "That's what scares me. What if I can't keep it separate?"

"Then you have to figure out if this thing with Evelyn is worth the risk," Becky said simply. "And if it is, you both need to be honest about it. No more dancing around the truth."

Cass nodded, even though Becky couldn't see her. "Thanks, Becky. I needed to hear that."

"Anytime, kid. Just remember, you've got this. No matter what happens."

Cass ended the call and stood there for a moment, the weight of Becky's words settling over her. She didn't have all the answers, but at least now she had a little more clarity.

When she walked back into the office, Evelyn was dressed and smoothing her hair, her professional mask firmly back in place.

"We should get going," Evelyn said, her tone brisk. "Busy day ahead."

Cass nodded, but as their eyes met, she saw the flicker of something unspoken lingering between them.

Cass stood in the doorway, her hand still on the knob, caught in the undertow of emotions she couldn't fully untangle. Evelyn's calm, professional demeanor had returned, and Cass felt a pang of frustration at how quickly she seemed to slide back into her armor. It wasn't fair, of course. Wasn't Evelyn entitled to protect herself, especially after the mess they'd just created? But that logical voice in Cass's head was drowned out by the roar of her own uncertainty.

She cleared her throat, stepping further into the room. "Evelyn," she began, her voice low, hesitant. "About what we said last night... What we did..."

Evelyn glanced up from where she was

adjusting her watch, her expression carefully neutral. "I know. It was a mistake."

The words landed like a punch to Cass's gut, and for a moment, she couldn't speak. She wasn't sure what she'd expected Evelyn to say, but hearing it framed so simply, so definitively stung more than she thought it would.

"A mistake?" Cass repeated, her tone sharper than she intended.

Evelyn's eyes flickered, betraying a crack in her composure. "I didn't mean it like that. I just—" She exhaled, her shoulders sagging slightly. "I don't know how to navigate this, Cass. I'm supposed to be impartial and focused on the job. Last night, it crossed every line."

"And you think I don't know that?" Cass shot back, the words spilling out before she could stop them. "You think I haven't been agonizing over the same damn thing? I've spent weeks fighting for this department, for my team, and now I'm supposed to figure out how to fight this"—she gestured vaguely between them—"whatever this is, without losing everything else in the process?"

Evelyn opened her mouth to respond,

then closed it again, her jaw tightening. For a long moment, neither of them spoke, the tension between them thick and suffocating.

Cass scrubbed a hand over her face, turning away. She stared at the pullout bed, now stripped of the intimacy it had held mere hours ago, and felt an overwhelming sense of loss.

"I'm not saying it wasn't real," Evelyn said quietly, breaking the silence.

Cass froze, her back still to Evelyn. The words hung in the air, fragile and tentative, like they might shatter if handled too carelessly.

"I'm saying I don't know how to make it work," Evelyn continued. Her voice was softer now, more vulnerable. "Not when we're still standing on opposite sides of this fight. I don't want to hurt you, Cass. But every decision I make, it feels like I'm doing just that."

Cass turned slowly, meeting Evelyn's gaze. For the first time, she saw something raw and unguarded there—regret, longing, fear.

"You're not the only one struggling with this," Cass said finally, her voice steady despite the storm inside her. "But maybe..." She hesitated, the words catching in her throat. "Maybe the problem isn't just us. Maybe it's everything around us. The expectations, the lines we're supposed to stay inside. Maybe we're letting all of that decide for us instead of figuring out what we really want."

Evelyn's expression softened, and for a moment, Cass thought she might agree. But then she shook her head, her lips pressing into a thin line. "I can't make promises I don't know if I can keep."

Cass felt her heart sink, but she nodded. "Neither can I."

They stood there, caught in the limbo between what they wanted and what they knew they could have. And as much as it hurt, Cass knew this was where they had to leave it for now.

∼

The tension in the meeting room was palpable as Cass sat at the long table with the other fire captains, her jaw tight and her hands clenched into fists beneath the surface. Evelyn stood at the head of the room, a stack of neatly organized documents in front of her and her usual air of professional detachment firmly in place. She looked calm, composed, and unshakable—the complete opposite of how Cass felt.

"This proposed restructuring," Evelyn began, her voice cutting through the room like a scalpel, "isn't about undermining your efforts or diminishing the importance of your work. It's about sustainability. The department is operating with outdated equipment and practices that, frankly, are no longer financially viable. If we don't act now, we'll be facing far more severe consequences in the future."

The other captains exchanged uneasy glances, but Cass couldn't hold back. "And if we make these cuts, what happens to response times? What happens when we're understaffed during a major incident because we're trying to save a few dollars?"

Evelyn didn't flinch, her gaze steady as she turned to Cass. "The proposed changes aren't about cutting corners. They're about optimizing resources. If we allocate funding more strategically, we can ensure—"

"Strategically?" Cass cut in, her voice rising. "You're talking about lives, Evelyn. You can't optimize a rescue. You can't calculate the worth of a life in dollars and cents."

The room grew quieter, the tension between them drawing everyone's attention. Evelyn's jaw tightened, and for the first time, there was a flicker of emotion in her eyes—anger, frustration, or something else Cass couldn't quite place.

"Captain Harris," Evelyn said evenly, her tone sharper now, "I understand your passion, but passion alone doesn't keep a department running. If we don't adapt to the realities of our budget, there won't *be* a department to protect anymore."

Cass pushed back her chair abruptly, standing. "Then maybe the problem isn't the department. Maybe it's the people who think they know better than the ones who actually do the work."

The other captains shifted uncomfortably, some murmuring in agreement, others remaining silent. Cass didn't care. She wasn't going to let Evelyn bulldoze over her team, her family, without a fight.

But even as the argument escalated,

something felt different. The usual fire that surged through Cass when she clashed with Evelyn wasn't there. Instead, every sharp word, every pointed glare felt like a blow to her chest.

Evelyn's lips parted, ready with another retort, but her gaze flickered over Cass's face, and for a split second, something softened. "I'm not your enemy, Cass," she said, her voice quieter now, though still firm. "I'm trying to find a way to make this work—for everyone."

Cass's anger faltered, replaced by a hollow ache she couldn't ignore. She sank back into her chair, the fight draining out of her. "It doesn't feel like it," she muttered, her voice barely audible.

The room fell into an uneasy silence, the weight of their words hanging heavy in the air. Evelyn glanced around, seeming to sense the shift in the atmosphere. She straightened, her professional mask slipping back into place like armor.

"We'll reconvene in a week," Evelyn said briskly, gathering her papers. "Take the time to review the proposals and come prepared with constructive feedback."

One by one, the other captains filed out of the room, some offering Cass sympathetic pats on the shoulder, others avoiding her gaze entirely. Evelyn lingered by the door, her expression unreadable.

Cass didn't look at her. She couldn't.

When the room was empty except for the two of them, Evelyn hesitated. "Cass—"

"Don't," Cass said, cutting her off. Her voice was flat, her eyes fixed on the table in front of her. "Just...don't."

Evelyn didn't respond. After a long moment, the soft click of the door signaled her departure.

Cass leaned back in her chair, staring at the empty room. She'd won plenty of arguments in her life, but this didn't feel like winning. It felt like losing something she wasn't sure she even had to begin with.

Her hands trembled as she rubbed her face, exhaustion pulling at her from every angle. She thought back to Becky's advice, to the firehouse, to Evelyn's lips against hers the night before. Every thought tangled together, creating a storm she couldn't control.

For the first time in her career, Cass felt like she was fighting a battle she couldn't win

—not because she wasn't strong enough, but because she wasn't sure which side she was supposed to be on anymore.

Cass sat slumped in her chair, the long table of the conference room stretching out in front of her like a chasm. The fluorescent lights overhead buzzed faintly, casting a harsh glare on the scattered papers and empty coffee cups left behind after the meeting. She stared at the spreadsheet in front of her, the columns and rows blurring into meaningless lines of text and numbers. Evelyn's voice still echoed in her head, calm and unyielding as she'd made her case for reallocating funds to other city initiatives.

The room was silent now, but Cass could still feel the tension hanging in the air, like smoke after a fire. Her chest ached, not from anger, but from something heavier, something she couldn't shake no matter how much she tried to convince herself otherwise.

It wasn't personal; she knew that. Evelyn wasn't doing this to hurt her, wasn't trying to dismantle the fire department out of spite or malice. If anything, Evelyn had gone out of her way to soften the blow of every cut, to find compromises that kept the department afloat. But knowing that didn't make it hurt any less.

Cass leaned back in her chair, rubbing her temples. "Damn it," she muttered to herself.

Their latest argument had been over something seemingly small—a line item in the budget for overtime pay. Cass had fought tooth and nail to protect it, arguing that the department relied on those funds to cover emergencies and to keep the team running when they were stretched thin. Evelyn had countered with her usual pragmatism, pointing out that the city simply didn't have the money to spare.

And so they'd gone back and forth, their voices rising, the tension between them crackling like a live wire. But this time, when the argument had ended and the others had filed out of the room, Cass hadn't felt the usual rush of righteous indignation, the fire that fueled her to fight harder for her team.

Instead, she'd felt...empty.

Her gaze drifted to the now empty chair where Evelyn had been sitting. Cass could still picture her there, her posture straight,

Playing with Fire

her hands clasped in front of her, her expression cool and composed. She'd barely raised her voice, but her words had cut through the room like a knife, precise and unrelenting.

Cass exhaled sharply, running a hand through her hair. It wasn't just the argument that was getting to her. It was the fact that every clash with Evelyn seemed to take a piece of her, leaving her more drained than the last.

Because it wasn't just a fight about money or resources. It was Evelyn.

The same woman who had held her in her arms not long ago, who had kissed her like she was the only thing in the world that mattered. The same woman whose laughter had filled Cass's office late at night, whose touch had made her feel alive in a way she hadn't felt in years.

And now they were here, on opposite sides of the table, their words sharp and cutting. Every argument felt like a betrayal, not because of what was being said, but because of who was saying it.

Cass dropped her head into her hands, her elbows braced on the table. "Why does this have to be so damn hard?" she whispered to no one.

She wanted to hate Evelyn in moments like this. It would be easier if she could. If she could convince herself that Evelyn was just another bureaucrat, another obstacle to overcome. But she couldn't. Because she knew Evelyn. She knew the woman who stayed up late poring over spreadsheets, trying to find solutions that worked for everyone. She knew the woman who carried the weight of the city on her shoulders, who took on the role of villain because someone had to.

But knowing didn't make it hurt less.

Cass stared at the table, her jaw tightening. She thought about her team—about Hallie, about Sara, about all the firefighters who relied on her to stand up for them, to fight for what they needed. She thought about Chief Thompson, who had trusted her to protect the department, to carry on the legacy she'd built.

And then she thought about Evelyn, about the way she'd looked at her during the argument. There had been something in her eyes, a flicker of something Cass couldn't quite recognize. Regret, maybe? Sadness? Or maybe Cass was just imagining it, projecting her own emotions onto someone who had never shown anything but resolve.

"Damn it, Evelyn," Cass muttered again, her voice thick with frustration.

She pushed back from the table, the chair scraping against the floor. She didn't know what to do with herself, didn't know how to reconcile the war inside her. How could she keep fighting when every battle left her feeling like she was losing no matter the outcome?

Her fists clenched at her sides as she paced the room. She wasn't angry at Evelyn, not really. She was angry at the situation, at the impossible choices they both had to make. She was angry at herself for letting her feelings get tangled up in the job, for caring too much about someone who was supposed to be her enemy.

But most of all, she was angry because she didn't know how to fix it.

Cass stopped at the window, looking out at the city below. The streets were quiet, the glow of the streetlights casting long shadows. Somewhere out there, Evelyn was probably sitting at her desk, poring over more spreadsheets, trying to find another way to make the numbers work.

And Cass? She was here, alone in a conference room, wondering how they'd gotten to this point.

For the first time in her career, she didn't feel like a leader, didn't feel like she had the answers. She felt...lost.

As she stared out at the city, her shoulders slumped, and a heavy sigh escaped her lips. She couldn't keep doing this—not like this. Something had to give.

But she didn't know what.

10

EVELYN

Evelyn stared blankly at the email on her computer screen, the neatly typed words blurring into an incomprehensible mess. She read them again, slower this time, as if giving them a second glance might somehow change their meaning. But the words remained the same, as cold and unyielding as the bureaucrats who had written them.

Directive from the City Finance Office: Effective immediately, the proposed reductions to staffing and equipment budgets for the Phoenix Ridge Fire Department must increase by 15%. Noncompliance will result in disciplinary action and a potential reassessment of departmental leadership.

Evelyn's stomach churned as the weight of the mandate settled over her. She pushed back from her desk, clasping her hands tightly in her lap in an effort to still their trembling. She had been bracing for bad news, but this? This was worse than anything she'd imagined.

The fire department was already operating at the edge of what she considered sustainable. Further cuts meant forcing Cass and her team to work with fewer resources, fewer people, and an even greater strain on their morale. It meant making sacrifices that Evelyn knew would cost lives—not just in the distant, statistical sense, but in the gut-wrenching reality of a firefighter standing in the wrong place without backup or proper gear.

And it meant facing Cass.

Evelyn pressed her palms against her temples, willing the pounding in her head to subside. She had spent weeks trying to find ways to mitigate the damage, poring over spreadsheets late into the night and arguing with city officials about priorities. She'd thought she could navigate this without destroying what little trust she had begun to build with Cass. Now, that hope seemed laughable.

A knock at the door jolted her out of her thoughts. Her assistant, Grace, poked her head in, her expression wary. "Ms. Ford? Everything alright?"

Evelyn forced herself to sit up straighter, smoothing her hands over her skirt. "Fine," she said, her voice clipped. "Just a lot to process."

Grace hesitated. "If you need me to reschedule your afternoon—"

"No," Evelyn interrupted. "I'll handle it."

The door closed softly behind Grace, leaving Evelyn alone with the suffocating quiet of her office. She clenched her fists, staring at the screen as if she could will the email out of existence. But no amount of denial would change what she had to do.

Cass's face swam into her mind, her fiery eyes and determined expression so vivid that it was almost as if she were in the room. Evelyn could practically hear her voice, sharp with frustration, accusing her of betrayal.

Evelyn buried her face in her hands. She didn't want to think about Cass. About the way she had felt, lying in Cass's arms the other night, their walls temporarily down. About the hope that had stirred in her chest, fragile and tentative, that maybe—just maybe—they could find a way to coexist. To be something more.

Evelyn leaned against the edge of her desk, staring at the stack of papers she'd brought with her to soften the blow, though she knew they'd do no such thing. She wasn't naive; she knew exactly how Cass would react. Every clash they'd had over the past few weeks had only confirmed what Evelyn already suspected: Cass Harris didn't just see arguments as professional disagreements. She took them personally, every single one. And this? This would feel like a betrayal.

It was in Cass's nature, Evelyn supposed. She was fiercely loyal to her team, to her station, to the ideals she believed in. To Cass, this wasn't just a fire department; it was her family, her legacy. Every decision Evelyn made was an attack on that, or at least that's how Cass saw it. Every policy shift, every budget cut—it all landed like a personal insult, as if Evelyn were targeting her specifically instead of trying to balance the needs of an entire city.

Evelyn sighed, pressing her fingers to her temples. She knew better than to expect Cass to see the bigger picture, but that didn't make this any easier. It wasn't just Cass's anger she feared; it was the way it lingered, a slow burn that didn't just die out after their arguments ended. Cass carried those feelings with her, letting them simmer just beneath the surface, fueling the next clash. And lately, Evelyn had felt that burn, too, though it ignited something far more complicated inside her—something she couldn't allow herself to name.

This time, though, it would be different. This wasn't a disagreement over protocol or priorities. This was about survival—the survival of the fire department, the city's budget, and Evelyn's own position. Cass wouldn't care about the reasons or the pressures Evelyn was under; she'd see it as proof that Evelyn didn't care about what mattered most.

And yet, Evelyn *had* to do it. There was no alternative. The weight of that reality pressed down on her like a leaden hand, the familiar pressure of duty clashing with the unfamiliar ache of knowing how much this would hurt someone she was starting to care about more than she should.

~

When Evelyn finally arrived at the firehouse that afternoon, she felt like she was walking into enemy territory. The usual hum of activity seemed muted, the weight of her impending conversation settling over the space like a storm cloud.

Cass was in the garage, overseeing a training drill. She was barking orders at her team, her tone sharp but not unkind. When she spotted Evelyn, her expression hardened, the faint smile she'd been wearing vanishing in an instant.

"Evelyn," Cass said, her voice cool. "What brings you here?"

Evelyn cleared her throat, her palms damp. "We need to talk. In private."

Cass's eyes narrowed, suspicion flashing across her face. "Alright," she said after a moment, nodding toward her office.

The walk to the office felt interminable, the silence between them heavy and oppressive. Evelyn's heels clicked against the floor, the sound unnaturally loud in the stillness.

Once inside, Cass closed the door and crossed her arms, leaning against the desk. "What's this about?"

Evelyn hesitated, her carefully rehearsed words evaporating under the weight of Cass's gaze. She looked at the woman in front of her, so strong and resolute, and for the first time, she felt a pang of genuine shame.

"There's been a directive from the city," Evelyn began, her voice softer than she intended. "The cuts...they're worse than we anticipated. We're being forced to increase reductions by fifteen percent."

Cass's expression darkened immediately, her jaw tightening. "You're joking."

"I wish I were." Evelyn forced herself to meet Cass's eyes. "This isn't what I wanted. I fought against it, but the decision's out of my hands now."

Cass's laugh was bitter, devoid of humor. "Out of your hands? That's convenient. You're the one delivering the orders, Evelyn.

Don't pretend you're some powerless messenger."

Evelyn flinched, the words cutting deeper than they should have. "Do you think this is easy for me?" she snapped, the crack in her composure surprising even herself. "Do you think I enjoy sitting in meetings with people who see this department as nothing more than a line item on a spreadsheet? I'm trying to make this work, Cass, but I can't perform miracles."

Cass pushed off the desk, her anger radiating from her in waves. "You're not trying hard enough. You're so busy playing by their rules that you've forgotten what's at stake. We're not numbers, Evelyn. We're people. And if you can't see that, then maybe you shouldn't be the one making these decisions."

The words landed like a blow, knocking the breath out of Evelyn's lungs. She took a step back, her hands trembling at her sides.

"Do you think I don't know that?" she said, her voice breaking. "Every decision I make keeps me up at night, wondering if I'm doing the right thing. But this isn't just about you or me or this department. It's about the entire city. And sometimes, doing the right thing means making impossible choices."

Cass shook her head, her anger giving way to something colder, more final. "No. The right thing is standing up for what's right, no matter how hard it is. If you can't do that, then I don't know what we're even doing here."

Evelyn felt the ground shift beneath her feet, the fragile connection they'd built crumbling before her eyes. "Cass..." She reached out instinctively.

Cass stepped back, her expression unreadable. "I can't do this anymore, Evelyn. I can't trust you—not with my department, and not with me."

The words hung in the air, a finality to them that made Evelyn's chest ache. She opened her mouth to respond, but no words came.

Cass turned and walked out, leaving Evelyn standing alone in the office, the silence deafening.

∼

Evelyn drove home in a daze, the city lights blurring past her. She gripped the steering wheel tightly, her knuckles white as she replayed the conversation over and over in her mind.

She had known this would happen. She had known that telling Cass about the cuts would drive a wedge between them, undoing whatever fragile bond they had managed to build. But knowing hadn't prepared her for how much it would hurt.

The house felt emptier than usual when she arrived, the quiet oppressive. Evelyn dropped her bag by the door and sank onto the couch, burying her face in her hands. She had spent her entire career keeping people at arm's length, building walls to protect herself from the pain of personal connections. She had thought she was good at it —until Cass.

Cass had torn through those walls with a force Evelyn hadn't anticipated, leaving her vulnerable in a way she hadn't been in years. And now, those walls felt like they were closing in on her, suffocating her with the weight of her own choices.

Evelyn stood alone in her living room,

the weight of silence pressing in on her from all sides. She stared at the papers in front of her, but they blurred together in a haze, unreadable and unimportant. Her mind kept drifting back to Cass, to their last exchange. It felt like an explosion had gone off in her chest, leaving her stunned and broken, every part of her aching from the force of it.

I never should have let it get this far.

The thought repeated itself like a mantra, echoing through the empty spaces of her mind. She had known the risks, of course. She had known the consequences of letting someone like Cass into her world, into the space where professional decisions and personal emotions never intersected. She'd always kept them separate—kept her guard up, her walls high. But somehow, somewhere along the way, she had allowed those walls to crack. Maybe it was the long hours spent arguing, the way Cass had been so fiercely passionate, so alive with conviction that had drawn Evelyn in. Or maybe it was the quiet moments when their gazes lingered a little too long or when Cass had said something that made Evelyn's heart flutter against her will. Either way, it didn't matter now.

I should've known better.

The truth, of course, was that Evelyn hadn't allowed herself to think about the consequences, hadn't let herself truly consider what would happen when the inevitable clash came. She had convinced herself it was manageable, that she could compartmentalize the relationship, keep it tucked neatly away from the professional decisions that needed to be made. But now, with the finality of their words hanging in the air between them, Evelyn realized how wrong she had been.

She never should have let herself care, never should have allowed that dangerous spark of attraction to turn into something more. The lines had been blurred from the start, and she'd been foolish enough to think she could navigate both worlds without them colliding. But they had. And now it had all come crashing down.

And it's my fault.

She couldn't look at the mirror without seeing the truth staring back at her. Cass had trusted her. She had opened herself up, even when Evelyn had been nothing but cold and distant. She had given her all, all while

Evelyn had been playing the role of the consultant, the outsider, the one who had to push through no matter the cost. Evelyn had pretended it was all part of the job. But it wasn't. Not really. She had let herself be swept up in something she wasn't prepared to handle. And now, everything was falling apart because of it.

Cass had made her choice. She'd drawn a line in the sand and told Evelyn that she couldn't be a part of this mess anymore. It was the logical conclusion, wasn't it? The breakup had been inevitable. And yet, Evelyn's chest ached with the raw, hollow emptiness left in the wake of Cass's departure. She had never felt so utterly alone.

I never should have let her in.

She wanted to scream, to do something —anything—to make it right again. But there was nothing to be done. Cass was right. She couldn't expect her to understand. The decisions Evelyn had to make weren't personal; they couldn't be. But that didn't matter. Cass had seen it that way. She'd taken everything personally, and Evelyn hadn't been strong enough to stop herself from letting it hurt.

Now there was nothing left. Just an empty home, a hollow ache in her chest, and the bitter taste of regret that Evelyn couldn't wash away.

For the first time in a long time, Evelyn felt the sting of tears at the corners of her eyes. She blinked them away, forcing herself to take a deep breath. She couldn't afford to fall apart now.

Cass's words echoed in her mind, sharp and unforgiving. *"I can't trust you."*

Evelyn closed her eyes, the ache in her chest spreading until it felt like it might consume her. She had always prided herself on her ability to remain composed under pressure, to make tough decisions without letting her emotions cloud her judgment.

But now, for the first time, Evelyn wasn't sure if she could.

11

CASS

Cass sat at her desk, the hum of the firehouse around her barely registering. The shift had started like any other, routine and predictable, yet everything felt off. She hadn't been able to focus on anything since the argument with Evelyn. No matter how hard she tried to pour herself into the work, the weight of everything that had happened pressed on her chest. It was like a constant, suffocating ache that wouldn't go away, no matter how much she tried to ignore it.

The day had been long, with multiple calls and briefings. The usual banter among the crew seemed distant, as if Cass were watching it all unfold through a fogged window instead of participating in it. She hadn't been able to connect with anyone—not the team, not Hallie, and definitely not Evelyn. It was like she was suspended in an emotional void, a place where nothing felt real anymore.

Her phone buzzed on the table, snapping her out of her spiraling thoughts. Hallie's name flashed across the screen, and Cass couldn't help but sigh before answering.

"Hey," Cass said, trying to keep her voice steady.

"Cass, you okay?" Hallie's voice was warm, concerned. There was a quiet understanding in it, the kind only a close friend could have.

Cass forced a smile, though Hallie couldn't see it through the phone. "Yeah. Just...tired. Long shift."

Hallie didn't buy it. There was a beat of silence on the other end of the line before Hallie spoke again, her voice quieter now, softer. "You've been distant. I get it. But you don't have to go through this alone."

"I'm fine," Cass replied, a little too quickly. She could feel the familiar defensive wall rising inside her, blocking out anything resembling vulnerability.

"Cass, come on. I've known you long enough to know when something's wrong. And you can't keep bottling everything up. Whatever's going on, you don't have to hide it from me," Hallie said gently, her concern clear.

But Cass only felt more closed off. She didn't want to talk about it—didn't want to admit the ache in her chest, the way her thoughts had been consumed by Evelyn ever since the breakup. The way she hadn't been able to get the image of Evelyn's eyes—shocked, devastated, cold—out of her head. The way every part of her wanted to reach out, to apologize, to fix what was broken, but pride and anger kept her rooted in place.

"I'm fine, Hallie," Cass repeated, her voice firm despite the storm brewing inside her. "I'll talk to you later."

The line went quiet as Hallie hesitated, sensing the finality in Cass's tone. "Okay," Hallie said after a moment, her voice a soft whisper. "But remember, I'm here if you change your mind."

Cass ended the call quickly, the weight of

Hallie's words hanging heavy in the air. She didn't want to admit it, but Hallie was right. Something was wrong. And no matter how hard she tried to bury it, it kept resurfacing. The image of Evelyn—the way she'd looked after their argument, the way she'd seemed so hurt by Cass's words—had become a permanent fixture in her mind.

It wasn't just the breakup that had torn her apart. It was everything that came with it. Cass had told herself that she had to choose between the firehouse and Evelyn, that one of them would have to go. And now she was left with nothing. Her team was at risk, the future of the department uncertain, and the one person who had made her feel something deeper than duty was no longer a part of her life.

She wanted to scream. She wanted to punch something. But instead, Cass buried herself in her work, throwing herself into training schedules, fire drills, and endless paperwork that never seemed to end. It was easier to focus on something tangible, something she could control. And maybe, just maybe, it would help her forget the wreckage of her own heart.

The days passed in a blur of routine. The firehouse felt emptier without the usual energy, without the tension that had sparked so much between her and Evelyn. Cass tried to push the lingering thoughts of Evelyn out of her mind, but they crept in at the most unexpected moments. During a briefing. While prepping for a call. When she was alone in her office, sitting at her desk. Evelyn's face haunted her—unbidden, unwelcomed, but undeniable.

The memories—their heated arguments, the passion that had simmered between them, the vulnerability they had both shared in their moments of closeness—only made her feel worse. She had pushed Evelyn away. She had been angry, hurt, and too stubborn to see the whole picture. And now, there was a part of her that regretted it.

But regret didn't change anything.

Cass stood in front of her team later that afternoon, talking through the schedule for the night shift, but her mind was a million miles away. The words felt foreign in her mouth, a hollow echo of what they used to mean. It was as if she were playing a part in a role she didn't quite believe in anymore. The firehouse had always been her purpose. But now, the fire inside her was flickering, weakening with every passing day without Evelyn.

The door to the room opened with a soft creak, and Cass instinctively turned her head, her heart leaping into her throat before she could even register who it was. Of course it wasn't Evelyn. It was Hallie, poking her head inside, looking concerned, as always.

"Cass, can we talk?" Hallie asked, stepping into the room with that same soft concern that had been there during their last conversation.

Cass glanced at her team. They were all focused, their attention diverted. She nodded, stepping away from the briefing to meet Hallie in the hallway.

"I didn't want to bug you," Hallie said quietly, once they were out of earshot. "But I can see something's eating at you. And I know you're trying to pretend it's not, but you're not fooling anyone."

Cass let out a short, humorless laugh. "You're the second person who's said that today," she muttered, running a hand through her hair. "I'm fine, Hallie. Just trying to get through this shift, okay?"

Hallie raised an eyebrow, clearly not buying it. "Cass, listen. I know you're tough, but that doesn't mean you have to do everything on your own. If you need to talk, you know I'm here."

"I just need to focus on the job," Cass snapped, frustrated with the emotions she couldn't quite manage. "That's all. So just drop it."

Hallie didn't say anything for a moment, then gently placed a hand on Cass's arm. "You know I'm not going to drop it, right?" she said, her voice low and understanding. "You can't just push everything down and expect it to disappear. If it's about Evelyn, it's okay to talk about it. You don't have to pretend like it's not affecting you. Because it is, and I can see it."

Cass flinched at the mention of Evelyn, her chest tightening. "I'm done with that," she said, her voice barely above a whisper. "I made my choice."

Hallie studied her for a long moment, then finally nodded, stepping back. "Okay. But just remember, you don't have to go through this alone. Whenever you're ready to talk, I'll be here."

Cass watched her leave, the weight of her words sinking deep inside her. She was right, of course. Cass had tried to bury everything, tried to focus on the firehouse and push aside what had happened with Evelyn. But she couldn't escape the truth. Even if she refused to admit it, a part of her was still tethered to that connection, still aching for something that had been torn away.

Maybe I made a mistake. The thought floated to the surface, uninvited but impossible to ignore.

But no matter how much she wanted to reach out, no matter how much she wanted to fix everything, she couldn't. Her pride wouldn't let her. She had made the decision. She had ended it. And she couldn't take it back now.

Or could she?

Cass turned her attention back to the firehouse, the noise, the orders, the routine. For now, it was all she had. But deep inside, she knew the fight for both the department and her own heart was far from over.

Cass sat at her desk in the quiet of the firehouse, the distant hum of the station's activities slipping through the cracks of her awareness. The weight of the morning's call had long since worn off, but it had been replaced by something heavier, darker. It wasn't the kind of weight that could be shaken off with a simple drink or a few hours of sleep. No, this was something deep within her—a slow, gnawing realization that she had lost everything.

She had lost Evelyn. That was the most glaring truth. Evelyn, the one person who had entered her life with the force of a storm, turning everything upside down. That moment in the office, the way they had collided felt so intense, so full of potential. Cass had let herself believe that despite the professional tension between them, despite all the walls they had put up, something real had sparked. But she had pushed it all away. She had told herself that it was the right thing to do, that she couldn't let personal feelings cloud her judgment, not when the future of the department was on the line.

She'd convinced herself that she could walk away from it, and now, every moment that passed seemed like another confirmation that she had made a mistake.

Evelyn was gone. The one person who had made her feel alive in a way she hadn't in years was slipping further away from her with every passing day. The anger, the pride, the bitterness—it had all clouded Cass's vision. And now, there was nothing left but the hollow ache of regret. Every argument, every sharp word she had thrown at Evelyn had only served to deepen the distance between them.

But that wasn't all she had lost.

She had lost her team. The people she had come to think of as family. They had always been her top priority—her rock, her responsibility. She had always prided herself on the way she led them, how they trusted her, how she protected them from the dangers of the job and the bureaucracy that threatened to tear them down. But now, Cass couldn't shake the feeling that she was failing them too. The department was on the verge of collapse. The cuts that Evelyn had insisted on were becoming inevitable.

Every time she saw a disappointed glance from one of her crew members, every time Hallie looked at her with concern, Cass felt like she was letting them down. They depended on her. They needed her to be strong, to be decisive, to stand up for them, and yet here she was, torn apart, lost in a mess of her own making. How could she protect them when she couldn't even protect herself?

And it wasn't just the department she was failing; it was the legacy of Chief Becky Thompson. The one person who had mentored her, who had believed in her, even when Cass hadn't believed in herself. Becky had trusted her to take up the mantle, to keep the department strong, to safeguard everything it stood for. But now, Cass felt like she was betraying her in the worst way possible.

Becky had always been there, steady and unshakeable, an example of what it meant to lead with honor and integrity. And Cass? Cass had been caught up in the mess of her emotions and her personal turmoil, letting everything she cared about slip away.

What would Becky think of me now? The

thought clawed at Cass's mind. She could practically hear Becky's voice in her head, that steady, no-nonsense tone telling her to snap out of it. To not let her emotions cloud her judgment, to focus on the job, to *protect* her team. But that was where Cass had failed. She had let her emotions get the better of her, let the pull of something personal distract her from the one thing she had always excelled at: her duty.

She had always believed that she could balance everything and that she could compartmentalize her personal life and her professional life. But now, it seemed so naive. How could she have thought that? How could she have been so blind to the truth— that everything she had worked so hard for could slip through her fingers so easily?

And worst of all, there was the lingering, gnawing fear that she might lose her job. With the cuts coming down the pipeline, with the city breathing down her neck, there was a real chance that her position as captain might be on the line. She had always prided herself on her leadership, but now, with the department in turmoil, with the weight of all these changes, she wasn't sure if she could hold on. Not if she couldn't hold it together. Not if she couldn't make the right decisions when it mattered the most.

The sense of helplessness was suffocating. There were too many things slipping out of her control, too many pieces falling apart. She didn't even know where to begin picking up the pieces. All she knew was that, right now, she couldn't see the way forward.

Cass stared out the window, the gray sky reflecting the heavy fog that clouded her mind. The city seemed distant and the streets empty, as though mirroring the emptiness she felt inside. She had tried so hard to be strong, to do the right thing, but now it felt like everything she had built was crumbling beneath her feet.

The station felt different these past few days—heavier, quieter. Her team had noticed the tension, though no one dared to ask what was wrong. They probably thought it was just the stress of the budget cuts looming over them, but Cass knew better.

The truth was, she was unraveling.

Her fingers drummed against the edge of her desk, the rhythm uneven, like her thoughts. She hadn't spoken to Evelyn since their fight, hadn't even seen her. Every time her phone buzzed, her stomach clenched, half-hoping it was Evelyn reaching out, half-hoping it wasn't. She'd buried herself in work, thinking if she stayed busy enough, she could avoid the gnawing ache in her chest. It wasn't working.

Cass leaned back in her chair, running a hand over her face. She felt raw, like an exposed nerve. The anger she'd felt that day had cooled, but it left behind something worse: doubt. She replayed the argument over and over in her mind, dissecting every word, every look, every pause.

Had she overreacted?

Part of her wanted to believe she hadn't. Evelyn had pushed for those cuts, knowing full well what they meant for the department. For her. Cass had every right to be furious. And yet...she couldn't shake the nagging feeling that maybe, just maybe, she hadn't let Evelyn explain. Hadn't given her the benefit of the doubt.

Her pride bristled at the thought. She didn't owe Evelyn anything, did she? After all, Evelyn was the one making decisions that put their team at risk. Evelyn was the one who had chosen to prioritize her job over their fragile, burgeoning connection.

But then Cass's gaze shifted to the framed photo on her desk—the team gathered in front of the station, all smiles and camaraderie. Her family. Her responsibility.

She exhaled a shaky breath, the weight of it all pressing down on her. She was supposed to protect them, to fight for them. And she was doing that, wasn't she? Pushing back against Evelyn, standing her ground, refusing to let the department be gutted?

But what if her anger had clouded her judgment? What if there was another way forward, but she'd been too stubborn, too hurt to see it?

Cass hated this feeling—this uncertainty, this vulnerability. She'd always prided herself on being decisive, on knowing exactly where she stood and what needed to be done. But now, everything felt tangled and messy. She couldn't separate her feelings for Evelyn from her anger over the cuts, couldn't untangle her frustration with the system from the ache of losing whatever it was they'd started to build together.

She glanced out the window, watching as

a couple of her firefighters walked across the lot, laughing about something. A pang of guilt twisted in her chest. They were counting on her. Every single one of them trusted her to stand up for them, to make sure they had what they needed to do their jobs safely.

And what have I done? She'd let her emotions get the better of her, stormed out, and slammed the door on Evelyn without even hearing her out. Now, days later, she wasn't any closer to a solution.

Cass leaned forward, resting her elbows on the desk and burying her face in her hands. She felt the familiar sting of tears threatening to spill and clenched her jaw against it. She didn't cry—not here, not where someone might walk in and see her.

But the pressure in her chest wouldn't ease, and the memories wouldn't leave her alone. She thought of Evelyn's face during their fight, the flash of something like hurt in her eyes, quickly masked by her usual calm exterior. Cass had been so angry, so sure of Evelyn's betrayal that she hadn't stopped to think about how it might feel for her.

She hated how Evelyn could get under

her skin like this, how she could make her doubt herself, make her question everything.

But what Cass hated most was the thought that maybe—just maybe—she'd let her pride ruin something that could've been good.

And Evelyn—god, Evelyn—would never forgive her. She knew that now. Cass had pushed her away when she should have held on. She had thrown away something precious, something that had meant more to her than she had been willing to admit.

But what could she have done? Cass didn't have the answers. All she knew was that it was too late now. Evelyn was gone, and she couldn't fix what she had broken. The firehouse was teetering on the edge of disaster, and Cass didn't know if she could pull it back from the brink.

What would Becky say to her now? Would she be proud of the choices Cass had made? Or would she see Cass for what she truly was: someone who had let everything slip away because she was too weak to make the hard choices?

Cass felt a tightness in her chest, a lump rising in her throat. She had failed. And she couldn't shake the feeling that there was no coming back from this.

She stood up abruptly, pacing back and forth in her office, as if moving would somehow push the thoughts away. But nothing would. She couldn't outrun the truth. It was right here, pressing in on her, crushing her from all sides.

Cass had tried to do the right thing. She had tried to be the captain her team needed, the leader that Becky had always seen in her. But somewhere along the way, she had lost her way. And now, she had nothing left to show for it but failure.

Her heart ached with the weight of it. She had lost everything.

And the worst part? She had no idea how to fix it.

12

EVELYN

Evelyn sat alone in her office, the stack of reports on her desk untouched. The city lights beyond the wide windows glittered in the darkness, but they only made the emptiness inside her feel sharper. She had spent the better part of the day in meetings, her professional mask firmly in place, but now that the quiet had descended, the weight of her choices pressed down on her with unbearable clarity.

Her gaze drifted to the photo on her desk, one of the department's community outreach days. Cass was in the background, laughing with one of the kids, her expression bright and unguarded. Evelyn swallowed hard and turned the frame face down, unable to look at it for another second.

For so long, Evelyn had lived her life by a single principle: control. She had built walls around herself so high and so thick that even she couldn't see over them. Vulnerability was a weakness, and weakness was something she couldn't afford—not in her career, not in her personal life. She had worked tirelessly to become the best at what she did, the one person people could count on to make the hard choices. But in doing so, she had shut herself off from the people who might have made all of it worth it.

And Cass...

Cass had been the one to breach those walls, not with careful persistence but with sheer force. She had challenged Evelyn in ways no one ever had, pushing back with a fire that had both infuriated and captivated her. Evelyn had told herself that it was nothing more than a professional clash, that the heat between them was just friction borne from opposing ideals. But that lie had crumbled the moment she had kissed Cass, the moment she had let herself feel.

Now, she was left staring at the ruins of

whatever fragile connection they had managed to build. And it was all her fault.

Evelyn leaned back in her chair, the leather creaking under her weight as she closed her eyes. She had thought she was protecting herself by keeping Cass at arm's length, by insisting on the lines they couldn't cross, by prioritizing her duty above all else. But in reality, she had been running. Running from the way Cass made her feel, the way she saw right through her, and the way she had made Evelyn want something more than just professional success.

It had all unraveled so quickly. The pressure from the city, the impossible decisions, the arguments that had spiraled into something raw and personal—it had pushed her into a corner. And when Cass had looked at her with that mix of anger and betrayal, Evelyn had felt something inside her break. She had told herself that it was better this way, that she was doing what needed to be done, but now, sitting here in the silence of her office, she couldn't escape the truth.

She had let fear win.

Evelyn opened her eyes, staring at the ceiling. She had spent her whole life avoiding vulnerability because she thought it made her strong. But now, all she felt was weak. Weak for pushing Cass away, for choosing control over connection, for clinging to the illusion that she could protect herself by keeping her distance.

Her phone buzzed on the desk, and she glanced at it, her heart sinking when she saw the message from the city manager. More updates on the budget cuts, more pressure to finalize the plans. Evelyn felt a surge of frustration, her fingers itching to hurl the device across the room. But she didn't. Instead, she set it down gently, her mind racing.

Was this really worth it? The accolades, the promotions, the spotless reputation—none of it seemed to matter anymore. Not when the cost had been Cass, not when she had destroyed the one thing that had made her feel alive in years.

For the first time in her life, Evelyn wasn't sure she could fix this. Cass had every right to hate her, to shut her out, to never forgive her. And yet, the thought of leaving things as they were—of walking away without trying—made Evelyn's chest tighten with a desperation she didn't know how to contain.

She didn't want to be this person anymore. She didn't want to let fear dictate her life, to keep running from the things that scared her. Cass had shown her that there was another way, that vulnerability wasn't the same as weakness, that connection could be a kind of strength she had never allowed herself to believe in.

But was it too late?

Evelyn stood, pacing the length of her office, her thoughts spiraling. She couldn't keep going like this, couldn't keep pretending that she was fine, that the decisions she had made were the right ones. Maybe it wasn't too late to change things. Maybe she could find a way to undo the damage she had done—not just to Cass, but to herself.

She stopped by the window, staring out at the city below. The fire station wasn't far, its familiar silhouette barely visible against the glow of the streetlights. She wondered if Cass was there now, pacing her own office, as tormented as Evelyn was. The thought sent a pang of longing through her, sharper than anything she had felt before.

Evelyn had always prided herself on her ability to stay composed, to never let her emotions interfere with her decisions. But now, for the first time, she wanted to let herself feel. She wanted to tell Cass the truth, to lay it all out, to take the risk she had been too afraid to take before.

She didn't know if Cass would forgive her. She didn't know if she could undo the choices that had driven them apart. But she had to try. Because if there was one thing Evelyn knew with absolute certainty, it was that losing Cass was a mistake she couldn't live with.

And for the first time in her life, Evelyn was ready to face her fear.

∽

Evelyn stared at her phone, the contact labeled *Becky Thompson* sitting at the top of her screen. She had been hovering over the call button for the better part of ten minutes, torn between her need for guidance and the stubborn pride that had kept her from asking for help for so long. Becky, legendary fire chief turned world traveler, had a reputation for cutting through the noise and getting to the heart of a problem. If anyone could give her clarity, it was Becky.

With a deep breath, Evelyn pressed the button and raised the phone to her ear. It rang twice before a familiar, warm voice answered.

"Evelyn Ford," Becky said, her tone amused. "I didn't expect to hear from you while I'm halfway across the world. What's the matter? The city council driving you mad or is it something worse?"

Evelyn hesitated, unsure how to begin. "Both," she admitted finally, her voice quieter than she intended.

Becky's tone softened. "Alright, kid. I'm in Italy sipping an espresso right now, so lay it on me. What's going on?"

Evelyn almost laughed at the mental image of the famously no-nonsense chief enjoying a leisurely afternoon abroad. But the weight of her situation quickly sobered her. "I think I've made a mess of everything, Becky."

There was a pause on the other end of the line, just long enough for Evelyn to feel the sting of her own admission. Then Becky's voice came, steady and patient. "Start from the beginning."

Evelyn sighed, dragging a hand through her hair as she sank into her office chair. "The city's been pushing me to make cuts to the fire department. Big ones. Necessary, they keep saying. I've been going back and forth with Cass Harris—the captain at Phoenix Ridge. You probably remember her."

"Cass? Of course I do," Becky said warmly. "She's got a fire in her, that one. Reminds me of myself when I was her age."

Evelyn smiled faintly at that. "Yeah, she does. She's been fighting me on every single change I've proposed. It's been...contentious. But somewhere along the way, things got complicated. We got involved—personally, I mean."

Becky let out a low whistle. "Well, now. That *is* complicated."

"I shouldn't have let it happen," Evelyn continued quickly, guilt threading through her words. "It was unprofessional, reckless. But I—" She broke off, unsure how to explain the pull Cass had on her, the way she had made Evelyn feel seen and challenged in a way no one else ever had.

"You care about her," Becky said gently, filling the silence. "Am I right?"

"Yes," Evelyn admitted, the word barely more than a whisper. "But it doesn't matter. I had to tell her about the cuts—cuts I don't even agree with but couldn't prevent. She took it as a betrayal, and I don't blame her. She ended things. And now, I've lost her, and I feel like I've lost myself in the process."

Becky was quiet for a moment, and Evelyn could almost hear the gears turning in her mind. Finally, she said, "Evelyn, you're one of the sharpest people I've ever worked with. You know how to read a situation, make the tough calls, and get results. But I think you've forgotten something important."

Evelyn frowned. "What's that?"

"You're not just fighting for the department or the budget or whatever agenda the city's pushing," Becky said. "Sometimes, the fight you need to win is for yourself. Not the job."

Evelyn leaned back in her chair, the

words hitting her with unexpected force. "What do you mean?"

"I mean, you've been so focused on doing what's expected of you—on being the professional, the fixer, the one who never falters—that you've lost sight of what you actually want," Becky said. "You want to save the department, sure. But you also want Cass. And you're afraid to admit that to yourself because it doesn't fit into the neat little box you've built for your life."

Evelyn's throat tightened. "It's not that simple."

"It never is," Becky agreed. "But let me tell you something I learned the hard way: If you keep choosing the job over your own happiness, you'll wake up one day and realize the job isn't enough. It won't hold you at night. It won't challenge you in ways that make you better. And it damn sure won't love you back."

Evelyn stared at the photo frame she had turned face down earlier, her heart aching. "I don't even know if she'd take me back," she admitted.

"That's not the point," Becky said firmly. "The point is whether you're willing to take the risk. Whether you're willing to fight for something that scares you, even if it means putting yourself out there."

Evelyn swallowed hard, the weight of Becky's words settling over her. "I don't know if I can."

"You can," Becky said, her voice unwavering. "You've got it in you, Evelyn. I've seen it. You've just got to get out of your own way. And if it doesn't work out? At least you'll know you gave it everything you had. But if you walk away now, without trying, you'll regret it. Trust me on that."

Evelyn closed her eyes, the fear and doubt swirling inside her. "I don't know where to start."

"Start by being honest," Becky said simply. "With yourself and with her. Tell her how you feel and what you want. It's scary, I know. But it's worth it."

Evelyn nodded slowly, even though Becky couldn't see her. "Thank you, Becky."

"Anytime," Becky said warmly. "And Evelyn? Don't forget, you're human. You're allowed to want things. Don't let anyone, least of all yourself, convince you otherwise."

The call ended, but Becky's words stayed

with Evelyn, echoing in the quiet of her office. She sat there for a long time, her thoughts churning. For the first time in years, she felt a flicker of something she hadn't allowed herself to feel in far too long: hope.

∼

Evelyn adjusted her blazer as she walked into the city council chambers, her heels clicking against the polished floor. The space felt cold, clinical—the kind of room designed to strip emotion from every decision. She glanced at the long conference table where the council members were already seated, their faces a mixture of impatience and disinterest. This was going to be an uphill battle, but she hadn't come this far to back down now.

Taking her seat at the end of the table, Evelyn spread her papers neatly in front of her. The proposed budget lay on top, its bold red highlights a glaring reminder of the cuts they had expected her to implement. Cuts that would gut the fire department. Cuts that would cost lives.

"Ms. Ford," Councilmember Graham began, adjusting his glasses as he looked over the papers in front of him. "We've reviewed your latest budget suggestions, and quite frankly, we're expecting more decisive action. The city's finances are non-negotiable."

Evelyn straightened her back, her expression calm but firm. "I understand the financial constraints, but the current proposal is not acceptable. It will compromise the department's ability to function effectively and put the community at risk. That's a line I won't cross."

Councilmember Patel, a sharp-eyed woman with a reputation for her no-nonsense approach, leaned forward. "Evelyn, we're not asking for your personal feelings on the matter. We're asking for solutions. If the fire department can't make these cuts, where do you propose we find the funding?"

Evelyn took a steadying breath, meeting Patel's gaze. "I have a proposal that avoids the drastic cuts while still addressing the budget deficit."

That got their attention. Graham raised an eyebrow. "We're listening."

Evelyn slid a packet of documents across

the table. "I've identified areas where we can redirect existing funds without sacrificing critical services. For one, the municipal fleet's vehicle replacement program can be deferred for a year. That alone frees up a significant portion of the budget."

Patel frowned. "The fleet program is already overdue. Those vehicles are barely holding up as it is."

"And yet," Evelyn countered, "the fire department has been making do with decades-old equipment. If they can manage, so can other departments. Additionally, I've spoken with private donors who are willing to contribute to the department's operating costs in exchange for increased visibility in community initiatives. It's not a permanent solution, but it buys us time to reassess priorities without resorting to layoffs or station closures."

There was a murmur of interest around the table. Councilmember Rivera, who had remained quiet until now, finally spoke. "Private donors? That's...unconventional."

"It's not ideal," Evelyn admitted, "but it's better than gutting a service that saves lives. The fire department isn't just a line item on a spreadsheet. It's the difference between life and death for the people in this city. I've spent weeks with them. I've seen their dedication. Cutting their resources would be a betrayal of everything they stand for."

The room fell silent. Graham tapped his pen against the table, his expression unreadable. "You're asking us to delay other critical programs and bring private money into public services. That's a hard sell."

Evelyn nodded. "I know it's not a perfect solution, but it's the only one that maintains the integrity of the fire department while addressing the financial realities we face. It's a compromise, but it's a fair one."

Patel leaned back in her chair, arms crossed. "And if this doesn't work? If the donors back out or the delays cause more problems than they solve?"

"Then we reassess," Evelyn said firmly. "But at least we'll have done everything possible to avoid irreversible damage to one of the city's most vital services."

The council members exchanged glances, their expressions skeptical but contemplative. Finally, Graham sighed, setting his pen down. "We'll consider it. But you'll need to justify every aspect of this plan and be prepared for pushback."

Evelyn's jaw tightened, but she nodded. "I understand. And I'm ready."

As the meeting adjourned, Evelyn gathered her papers and walked out of the chamber, her heart pounding. She had stood her ground, but she knew the fight wasn't over. Still, for the first time in weeks, she felt like she had taken a step in the right direction.

Now, she just had to see if Cass would believe in her too.

∽

Evelyn stood outside the firehouse, her heart pounding like it hadn't in years. The building loomed before her, all brick and grit, a testament to the lives it protected and the people who gave everything to serve the community. She had spent the past few days pulling off what felt like a miracle—hours of negotiation, phone calls, and favors called in from old allies. Against all odds, she had done it. The department wouldn't face the cuts, at least not the devastating ones initially planned.

But now, standing here, on the threshold of making things right with Cass, she felt the weight of a very different kind of risk.

Taking a steadying breath, she smoothed her blazer, tucked a strand of hair behind her ear, and pushed open the door. The familiar scent of smoke and leather greeted her, mingled with the faint hum of activity in the background. She spotted a few firefighters in the bay, but her eyes immediately searched for the one person she was here to see.

13

CASS

Cass rubbed her temples, the tension in her head threatening to bloom into a full-blown migraine. The clock on the wall ticked relentlessly, reminding her of all the time she'd spent hunched over reports, budgets, and endless proposals for alternative funding. She was running on fumes, her meals replaced by cups of stale coffee and whatever snacks the crew left lying around the station. Sleep was an afterthought, snatched in fleeting moments between strategy sessions and restless nights filled with too many regrets. Her body protested every movement, muscles sore from the constant grind, but she couldn't stop—not when her team was counting on her.

Her desk was a mess: stacks of papers with scribbled notes, emails she'd printed out in desperation, and crumpled drafts of pleas she'd considered sending to the city council. Cass was determined to find a solution, anything to avoid the devastating cuts Evelyn had warned about. Yet the harder she fought, the more it felt like she was swimming against a relentless current. She couldn't shake the hollowness that had settled in her chest, a gnawing grief that had nothing to do with the department and everything to do with Evelyn. It was as if the fight for her team and the fight for her heart had merged into one unbearable battle. She was staring blankly at the paperwork in front of her. The words blurred together, her mind too weighed down by the steady ache in her chest. She'd barely slept the past few nights, her dreams haunted by Evelyn's face, her sharp words from their last conversation echoing like a cruel refrain. Evelyn was the last person she expected—or wanted—to see, and yet she was the only one Cass couldn't stop thinking about.

A knock at the door broke through her haze.

"Yeah?" she called, not bothering to look up.

The door opened, and she froze when Evelyn's voice followed. "Cass, can we talk?"

Cass's head snapped up, her heart doing an uncomfortable lurch in her chest. Evelyn stood there, a stack of papers in her hand, her expression guarded but earnest. She wore one of her crisp blazers, her usual armor of professionalism, but her eyes gave her away. There was something vulnerable in them, a hesitation Cass wasn't used to seeing.

"What are you doing here?" Cass asked, her voice sharper than she intended. She leaned back in her chair, crossing her arms. "I thought we said everything we needed to say."

Evelyn stepped inside, shutting the door behind her. "I know. But I needed to tell you something—something I should've told you sooner."

Cass raised an eyebrow, waiting. Her defenses were already up, her walls built high. But Evelyn didn't flinch under her scrutiny. Instead, she crossed the room, setting the papers down on Cass's desk.

"I fought back," Evelyn said quietly. "Against the cuts. I refused to make the changes they wanted."

Cass blinked, her arms uncrossing slightly. "What?"

Evelyn straightened her shoulders, her voice steady. "The city council wanted me to gut the department, to slash resources in ways that would have left you and your team vulnerable. I said no. I found an alternative. It's not perfect, but it's enough to keep you operational—more than operational."

Cass stared at her, the words not fully registering at first. "You...what?"

"I found private donors willing to invest in the department," Evelyn explained. "And I convinced the council to redirect funds from other areas. It took some convincing, but I wouldn't leave until they agreed. The cuts are off the table, Cass."

The weight of those words sank in, but

Cass didn't feel the immediate relief she thought she would. Instead, she felt an overwhelming mixture of emotions—shock, gratitude, confusion, and a lingering anger she didn't know how to shake.

"Why?" she asked, her voice low. "Why would you do that?"

Evelyn's gaze faltered for the first time. She hesitated, as if weighing whether or not to say what was truly on her mind. "Because I couldn't live with myself if I didn't. Because you were right, Cass. About everything. And because... I couldn't stand the thought of losing you."

Cass's breath caught in her throat. Evelyn looked so different now, her usual cool composure cracking at the edges. Her vulnerability was like a spotlight, illuminating every unspoken truth between them.

"You didn't lose me," Cass said softly, though her voice was thick with emotion. "I'm still here. But you, Evelyn, you broke my trust. I don't know if I can forget that."

Evelyn nodded, her expression pained. "I know. I messed up, Cass. I made decisions out of fear—fear of failing, fear of...feeling anything I couldn't control. But I've realized something." She took a deep breath, her voice trembling slightly. "Being around you, seeing how much you care about your team, your work—it's changed me. I thought I could keep everything in neat little boxes, but I can't. Not with you."

Cass looked away, her throat tight. She wanted to believe Evelyn, but her anger and hurt hadn't fully healed. "This isn't just about us, Evelyn. This is about my team. My family. If you'd gone through with those cuts..."

"But I didn't," Evelyn interrupted gently. "I fought for them, Cass. I fought for you. And I'll keep fighting, if you'll let me."

Cass's heart ached at the sincerity in Evelyn's voice. She wanted to stay angry, to hold on to the betrayal. But as she looked at Evelyn—truly looked at her—she saw the woman who had stood her ground against the council, who had taken a risk to protect something she didn't fully understand but knew was important. She saw the woman she couldn't seem to stay away from, no matter how hard she tried.

"You really mean that?" Cass asked, her voice barely above a whisper.

Evelyn stepped closer, her gaze unwavering. "Yes. I can't promise I won't make mistakes, Cass. But I promise I'll always try to do what's right. For you. For the department."

The vulnerability in her voice shattered something inside Cass. She stood, closing the distance between them, her hands resting on her hips as she searched Evelyn's face for any sign of insincerity. She found none.

"You drive me crazy, you know that?" Cass said, her voice breaking into a soft laugh, though tears shimmered in her eyes. "I've never met anyone who could make me this angry and this..."

"This what?" Evelyn asked, her voice barely audible.

Cass hesitated, then let out a shaky breath. "This alive. Damn it, Evelyn, I hate how much I care about you."

Evelyn's lips quirked into a faint, bittersweet smile. "I hate it too," she admitted. "But I think that's what makes it real."

Cass shook her head, laughing softly despite herself. "You're impossible."

"And you're infuriating," Evelyn countered, though her tone was light, almost teasing. "But maybe that's why this works."

They stood there for a moment, the tension between them replaced by something softer, something fragile but hopeful. Cass finally reached out, her hand brushing against Evelyn's. Evelyn took it, her grip firm but gentle, and for the first time in weeks, Cass felt a sense of peace.

"Okay," Cass said finally. "Let's see where this goes. But if you pull another stunt like that, I'm kicking your ass."

Evelyn laughed, the sound warm and genuine. "Fair enough."

It wasn't a perfect resolution, but it was a start. And for now, that was enough.

Cass stared at Evelyn, her pulse roaring in her ears. The warmth of Evelyn's hand in hers was grounding, but it did little to stop the storm of emotions churning inside her. Anger, hurt, hope, and something even deeper tangled together, leaving her breathless. She hadn't realized how much she had been holding on to, how tightly the tension between them had gripped her heart, until now. Until Evelyn was standing here, vulnerable and open in a way that felt impossible just weeks ago.

Cass didn't know who moved first. One moment, they were standing inches apart, the air between them thick with unsaid words and raw emotions; the next, Evelyn was closer, her gaze flickering to Cass's lips, her breath mingling with Cass's. It was a silent question, and Cass knew her answer before she even realized she was leaning in.

Their lips met in a kiss that was nothing like the ones before. Those had been heated, frantic, and borne of frustration and pent-up desire. But this...this was slow, deliberate, and achingly tender. Cass felt the weight of everything they had been through in that moment, all the arguments, the betrayals, the undeniable pull that had brought them together despite everything working to keep them apart.

Evelyn's hand slid up to Cass's cheek, her touch soft and careful, as if she were afraid to break the fragile peace between them. Cass tilted her head, deepening the kiss, her own hands moving to Evelyn's waist. She pulled her closer, feeling the warmth of her body, the steady thrum of her heartbeat against her own.

A sigh escaped Cass, unbidden, as relief flooded through her. For weeks, she had been carrying so much—resentment, confusion, guilt, longing. It had weighed her down, creeping into every corner of her life, until she felt like she might drown under it all. But here, with Evelyn in her arms, the pressure lifted, replaced by something softer, something lighter. It wasn't perfect, and the hurt wasn't entirely gone, but for the first time in what felt like forever, Cass could breathe.

Evelyn broke the kiss first, her forehead resting against Cass's, her eyes closed. Her breathing was uneven, her lips slightly parted, and Cass felt her chest tighten at the sight. Evelyn looked different now, her usual cool composure stripped away, leaving her vulnerable and real in a way Cass had never seen before.

"I'm sorry," Evelyn murmured, her voice shaky but sincere. "For everything. For hurting you."

Cass's thumb brushed against Evelyn's cheek, wiping away a tear she hadn't even noticed. "You don't have to keep apologizing," she said softly, her own voice rough with emotion. "You fixed it, Evelyn. You stood up for us, for what's right. That's what matters."

Evelyn's eyes opened, meeting Cass's, and Cass saw something there she hadn't expected—hope. It was tentative, fragile, but it was enough to make Cass's heart ache. She leaned in again, pressing another kiss to Evelyn's lips, this one softer, gentler, a promise rather than a demand.

The kiss deepened slowly, naturally, their movements unhurried as if they had all the time in the world. Cass let herself get lost in the moment, in the feel of Evelyn's lips moving against hers, the warmth of her body pressed close, the faint scent of her perfume mingling with the lingering smell of coffee in the office. It wasn't just a kiss; it was a release, a way to let go of everything that had been weighing them down and start fresh.

As they broke apart again, Cass rested her forehead against Evelyn's, her hands still on her hips. She let out a shaky laugh, her breath fanning across Evelyn's skin. "This feels...different," she admitted, her voice barely above a whisper.

Evelyn nodded, her fingers curling gently around the front of Cass's shirt. "Because it is," she said. "It's not just heat or tension or any of that. It's more."

Cass swallowed hard, her throat tight with emotion. She had spent so long trying to fight what she felt for Evelyn, convincing herself it was just physical attraction or misplaced frustration. But standing here now, holding Evelyn, she couldn't deny the truth any longer. It wasn't just about the way Evelyn challenged her or the spark between them. It was about the way Evelyn had stepped up, had fought for what mattered, even when it wasn't easy. It was about the way Evelyn had seen her, really seen her, and hadn't looked away.

"I'm scared," Cass admitted, the words slipping out before she could stop them. "I'm scared this won't work. That we'll screw it up. That I'll screw it up."

Evelyn's hand came up to cup Cass's face, her thumb brushing lightly over her cheek. "Me too," she said quietly. "But I think...I think it's worth the risk."

Cass stared at her for a long moment, letting those words sink in. Worth the risk. She thought about all the things she had already risked for this, for them. Her pride, her anger, her fear. And now, standing here with Evelyn, she realized she would do it all again if it meant holding on to this, on to her.

Without thinking, Cass pulled Evelyn into another kiss, this one filled with all the emotion she couldn't put into words. It was a kiss of gratitude, of forgiveness, of hope. Evelyn responded in kind, her arms wrapping around Cass's neck, holding on like she never wanted to let go.

When they finally broke apart, both of them breathing heavily, Cass rested her hands on Evelyn's shoulders, her forehead pressed against hers. She let out a soft, breathless laugh, her lips curving into a small smile.

"Guess we're really doing this, huh?" she said, her voice light but filled with meaning.

Evelyn smiled back, her eyes shining with something that looked an awful lot like happiness. "Yeah," she said. "I guess we are."

For the first time in weeks, Cass felt something other than anger or frustration or despair. She felt hope. It wasn't perfect, and it wouldn't be easy, but as she held Evelyn close, she knew one thing for certain—they were worth fighting for.

∿

Cass leaned back against the edge of her desk, crossing her arms as she looked at Evelyn. The tension between them had finally broken, replaced by a fragile calm. Evelyn stood nearby, smoothing down her shirt with a nervous energy that was out of place for her usually composed demeanor. For a moment, they just looked at each other, as if testing the waters of this new, uncharted territory they'd stepped into.

"So," Cass began, breaking the silence. She let the word hang in the air, unsure of how to follow it up. What was the protocol for addressing...whatever this was?

Evelyn quirked an eyebrow, a faint smile tugging at the corner of her lips. "So," she echoed, her voice soft but tinged with amusement. "Are we going to talk about what happens now or just keep staring at each other like this?"

Cass huffed a laugh, running a hand through her hair. "Yeah, I guess we should, you know, figure out how to not completely screw this up."

Evelyn's smile widened slightly, and she stepped closer, leaning one hip against the desk beside Cass. "I think step one is acknowledging we've already screwed it up a little," she said, her tone light but honest. "Not exactly a textbook example of professionalism."

Cass tilted her head, feigning deep thought. "You mean arguing in front of half the department, nearly tackling each other in the middle of budget meetings, and, well, the other stuff wasn't professional?" She smirked when Evelyn rolled her eyes.

"I'm serious, Cass," Evelyn said, though her smile remained. "This is...complicated. We have to be careful."

"I know," Cass admitted, her smirk fading into something softer. She looked down at her hands, her fingers fidgeting with the edge of her desk. "It's not like I don't think about it. Every time I walk into this firehouse, I'm reminded that these people—my team—they depend on me. On us. I can't let them down."

Evelyn's expression softened, and she placed a hand on Cass's arm. "And you won't," she said firmly. "You've been fighting for them since the day we met. Honestly, you've reminded me why I wanted this job in the first place. It's not just numbers or policies. It's people."

Cass looked up, her eyes meeting Evelyn's. There was no hesitation there, no hidden agenda, just sincerity. She let out a slow breath. "Okay," she said. "So, what's step two? After admitting we're already in over our heads."

Evelyn tilted her head, pretending to think. "Step two is boundaries," she said. "We need to figure out how to separate work and...whatever this is."

Cass raised an eyebrow. "Boundaries, huh? Does that mean no more yelling at each other in meetings?"

"Preferably," Evelyn said dryly. "Though I won't promise I won't still push your buttons from time to time."

Cass chuckled, shaking her head. "You're impossible, you know that?"

"And you're stubborn," Evelyn countered, her smile teasing. "Guess we'll call it even."

They shared a laugh, the kind that came easily now that the tension between them had eased. It felt strange but good, like stepping into a room filled with sunlight after being in the dark for too long. Cass reached out, taking Evelyn's hand in hers.

"Look," Cass said, her voice softening. "I know this isn't going to be easy. We're both used to doing things our way, and this is new for both of us. But I'm willing to try if you are."

Evelyn squeezed her hand, her gaze steady. "I am. I know it won't be perfect, but I'm not willing to walk away from this. From you."

Cass felt a warmth spread through her chest at Evelyn's words, a mix of relief and something deeper. "Alright," she said, her lips curving into a small smile. "But just so you know, if you try to sneak any more budget cuts past me, we're going to have a problem."

Evelyn laughed, a sound that was light and genuine. "Noted. I'll make sure to give you a full breakdown in advance."

"You'd better," Cass teased, though her tone was affectionate. She leaned in slightly, her voice dropping to a mock-serious whisper. "And no more kissing me in the middle of arguments."

Evelyn arched an eyebrow, her smile turning sly. "I don't recall you complaining at the time."

Cass groaned, shaking her head. "You're impossible," she muttered, though the smile tugging at her lips betrayed her.

"And you like it," Evelyn replied, her tone playful but her eyes warm.

For a moment, they just stood there, the weight of their conversation balanced by the lightness of their banter. Cass felt a sense of ease she hadn't in weeks, a sense that maybe, just maybe, they could figure this out together. She squeezed Evelyn's hand once more before letting go.

"Okay," Cass said, straightening. "Let's give this a shot. Professionally and personally. But if it gets too messy, we talk it out. Deal?"

"Deal," Evelyn said, her smile soft but sure. She extended her hand, her expression serious but tinged with humor. "To clear communication and fewer arguments?"

Cass laughed, shaking Evelyn's hand. "To trying not to kill each other, at least."

They both laughed, the sound filling the room with a sense of possibility. Cass knew they had a long road ahead, but for the first time, she felt like they were on the same page. And that, she thought, was a damn good start.

EPILOGUE

5 YEARS LATER

Evelyn adjusted the lapels of her blazer, glancing out the wide glass windows of the city administration building as the late morning sun streamed in. The meeting had gone well—another discussion about expanding public safety programs into underfunded neighborhoods, one of the many initiatives she'd championed in her new role overseeing public safety for the city. It was satisfying work, work that mattered, but it didn't consume her the way her old position had.

For years, Evelyn had defined herself by her job. The endless spreadsheets, the meticulously plotted budgets, the need to prove herself capable in every room—all of it had been her armor, her way of controlling a world that could often feel chaotic. Now, the edges of that armor had softened. She still loved structure and efficiency, but she'd learned to let a little mess in too. Life was richer for it.

As she packed up her notes and slid them into her briefcase, Evelyn thought back to how she'd resisted this role at first. When the mayor had suggested she shift her focus away from direct budget oversight, it had felt like a demotion, like she was being sidelined. But Cass, ever the pragmatist, had seen it differently.

"This is your chance to shape the big picture," Cass had said one night as they sat on their porch, Smokey, their dog, sprawled at their feet. "You're not losing influence; you're gaining freedom. And honestly? Maybe you don't need to fight every battle head-on anymore."

Evelyn had scoffed at the time, but Cass had been right. As always.

She smiled faintly, thinking of Cass. Her wife—Evelyn still sometimes marveled at the word—had a way of grounding her in the best possible way. Where Evelyn's mind tended to spiral with possibilities and contingencies, Cass had a gift for cutting through the noise, for reminding her what really mattered. It wasn't that Evelyn loved her work any less now; it was that she no longer felt the need to carry the weight of the world on her own.

The phone on her desk buzzed, pulling her from her thoughts. She picked it up to see a text from Cass:

"BBQ at the station this weekend. Don't forget to pick up the buns this time. "

Evelyn rolled her eyes affectionately and typed back:

"One time. I forgot them one time. "

Their banter was effortless now, a rhythm they'd found over the years. Evelyn remembered how rocky their beginning had been—how every argument had felt like a battlefield, every glance a challenge. And yet, beneath all that fire, they'd found something neither of them had expected: peace.

Sliding her phone back into her pocket, Evelyn stood and grabbed her briefcase. She had a lunch meeting with a coalition of community leaders in an hour, but for now, she allowed herself a moment to soak in the quiet satisfaction of her new life.

As she walked down the corridor toward the elevator, Evelyn reflected on how different she felt these days. She still took her work seriously—it was important, after all—but she no longer defined her worth by her job. She had things outside of work now: shared evenings with Cass, weekend hikes with Smokey, the chaotic joy of their annual firehouse BBQs. She'd even taken up yoga, though Cass insisted her precision-obsessed brain made her look hilariously rigid in every pose. Evelyn took the teasing in stride; it was part of the give-and-take that made their life together so full.

The elevator doors slid open, and Evelyn stepped inside, greeting a few colleagues with a polite nod. She was still professional to her core, but she no longer felt the need to be the coldest, sharpest person in the room. In fact, she'd started to enjoy surprising people with the occasional joke or warm smile. Cass claimed it made Evelyn less intimidating, though Evelyn wasn't entirely convinced.

As the elevator descended, Evelyn's mind

drifted back to Cass again. She thought about the way Cass lit up when she talked about her team, the pride she took in mentoring the younger firefighters. Cass's work wasn't easy, but she poured her heart into it, just as Evelyn had learned to do in her own way. Together, they'd found a balance—a partnership that worked because they respected each other's passions.

When the elevator doors opened, Evelyn strode into the lobby, her heels clicking against the marble floor. A familiar sense of purpose filled her as she stepped out into the sunshine, but it was different now. The purpose wasn't about proving herself or controlling everything; it was about making a difference and still having time to enjoy the life she'd built with Cass.

She stopped at a coffee cart on the corner and ordered an iced latte, the barista recognizing her and chatting briefly about a recent city initiative. Evelyn engaged easily, realizing how much she'd changed. The old Evelyn would have kept the conversation brisk, polite but distant. Now, she found herself genuinely interested, grateful for the connection.

As she sipped her coffee and walked toward her next meeting, Evelyn felt a deep sense of gratitude. She still had ambitions, still cared about her work, but it no longer consumed her. She had Cass, their little corner of the world, and a life that felt, for the first time, whole.

For a woman who'd once believed she had to keep herself separate to stay strong, that realization was everything.

∼

The familiar clang of the station bell echoed through the bay, signaling a new shift. Cass Harris stood near the truck, clipboard in hand, watching her crew as they moved with practiced ease. She had seen this routine play out hundreds of times over the years, but it never grew old. Every roll call, every drill, every call-out reminded her why she had fought so hard for this team, why she continued to pour her heart into the station.

Cass was no longer just *Captain Harris;* she was a symbol of resilience for the Phoenix Ridge Fire Department. Her team teased her about it sometimes, calling her *"the legend of Phoenix Ridge."* But Cass didn't feel like a legend. She was just a firefighter, doing what needed to be done.

"Alright, let's tighten this up!" she called, clapping her hands to draw everyone's attention. "Masie, you're still favoring your right side on the hose advance. Center your stance or you'll end up flat on your ass when the water kicks in."

Masie, a rookie barely six months in, flushed but nodded, quickly adjusting her posture. Cass nodded back, hiding her smile. She saw potential in the kid, even if she tripped over her own boots sometimes. It was moments like these that reminded her of herself, back when Becky Thompson had stood in her place.

Becky. The thought of her old mentor brought a swell of bittersweet nostalgia. Becky had been a force of nature, a leader who had somehow managed to inspire and intimidate in equal measure. Cass still remembered the first time Becky had barked at her for a sloppy ladder climb during training. She'd been mortified, but it had driven her to work harder, to prove herself.

And now, here she was, passing on the

same lessons. Cass's leadership style was different—less barking, more guiding—but the core values were the same. Accountability. Teamwork. Pride in the badge.

"Alright, let's take five," Cass said, waving the group toward the break area. As the team dispersed, she caught sight of Masie lingering by the truck, clearly stewing over her earlier critique. Cass approached her, leaning casually against the rig.

"Hey, Masie, you're doing good work out there," she said, her tone softer now. "But you've gotta trust your body to do the job. It's not just about strength; it's about balance and instinct. You'll get there."

Masie looked up, her expression a mix of relief and determination. "Thanks, Cap. I'll keep working on it."

Cass nodded, clapping her on the shoulder. "Good. That's all I ask."

She watched Masie join the others, a quiet sense of pride settling over her. Mentoring wasn't just about teaching skills; it was about building confidence and helping people see their potential. Becky had done that for her, and now it was her turn to do it for others.

The sound of boots on the bay floor drew her attention, and she turned to see Hallie approaching. Her co-captain and closest friend, Hallie, had been by her side through the station's toughest years.

"You're getting soft, Cap," Hallie teased, jerking her thumb toward Masie. "Becky would've chewed her out until she couldn't tell left from right."

Cass smirked. "Yeah, well, Becky also threw coffee mugs when she was mad. I think we can modernize a little."

Hallie chuckled. "Fair point. Still, you've got a way with them. These rookies would run through fire for you."

Cass shook her head, the praise making her a little uncomfortable. "They'd do it for the team, not for me. That's what matters."

Hallie studied her for a moment, her expression softening. "You've built something special here, Cass. Don't downplay it."

Cass didn't respond immediately. Instead, she glanced around the bay, taking in the sight of her team joking and laughing as they hydrated and prepped for the next drill. It wasn't just a job to her; it was family. And she'd do anything to protect them.

The sound of a familiar ringtone cut through the background noise, and Cass pulled her phone from her pocket. It was Becky, calling from yet another exotic location. She grinned, answering with a playful, "Shouldn't you be off sipping wine in Tuscany or something?"

Becky's warm laugh came through the line. "I'll have you know I'm in Scotland this week. Whiskey, not wine."

"Living the dream, huh?" Cass leaned against the truck, already feeling the comfort of her mentor's voice.

Becky's tone turned knowing. "And how's life in Phoenix Ridge? Keeping those rookies in line?"

"Trying to," Cass said with a chuckle. "They're a good group. Reminds me of us back in the day."

"Poor souls," Becky quipped, then added more seriously, "You're doing good work, Cass. I hear nothing but praise about you and your team."

Cass hesitated, the weight of those words settling on her. "Thanks, Becky. That means a lot."

"It should," Becky said firmly. "You've

earned it. And don't forget—you've got a life outside that station too. Don't let the job swallow you whole."

Cass glanced toward the break area, where her team was starting to reassemble for the next drill. Becky's advice stayed with her, a reminder of the balance she was still learning to maintain. She had the job, yes, but she also had Evelyn, their dog Smokey, and the little world they'd built together.

After hanging up with Becky, Cass straightened and called out, "Alright, break's over! Let's see if Mia can keep her balance this time."

The team groaned and laughed as they fell into formation, ready for the next challenge. Cass watched them with a mix of pride and gratitude, knowing that the legacy she'd been entrusted with was in good hands. And as she stepped back into the rhythm of her day, she felt the unshakable certainty that she was exactly where she was meant to be.

∽

The sun was dipping low on the horizon, painting the Phoenix Ridge skyline in hues of orange, pink, and gold. Cass leaned back in her rocking chair on the porch, her boots propped up on the rail. Smokey, their perpetually sleepy rescue dog, was sprawled at her feet, his tail twitching lazily as he dreamed. Beside her, Evelyn sat with a glass of wine in hand, the soft light catching the streaks of silver in her hair.

Their house, perched just outside the bustle of the town, was quiet, save for the occasional chirp of crickets and the whisper of the wind through the trees. It was a far cry from the chaos that had once dominated their lives, but neither of them missed the noise.

"How was your meeting today?" Cass asked, breaking the comfortable silence. She glanced sideways at Evelyn, who was absently swirling her wine.

Evelyn let out a small laugh, tilting her head back against the chair. "Oh, you know. The usual dance of politics and diplomacy. We spent an hour debating the font size on a public safety pamphlet. Riveting stuff."

Cass smirked. "Sounds like you're really changing the world."

"Don't mock me," Evelyn said, her voice teasing. "I'll have you know that pamphlet might save lives. If anyone ever reads it."

Cass chuckled, reaching down to scratch behind Smokey's ears. "Well, for what it's worth, I think you're doing good work. Even if it's in Helvetica."

Evelyn rolled her eyes but smiled, her fingers brushing lightly against Cass's arm. "And you? Did you terrorize any rookies today?"

"Not terrorize," Cass corrected with a mock-serious tone. "Mentor. I'm shaping the future of firefighting, one awkward hose drill at a time."

Evelyn arched a brow. "And how's Masie doing? Has she figured out which end of the hose to hold yet?"

Cass snorted. "Barely. But she's got heart, and that counts for something."

They sat in silence for a moment, the kind of silence that didn't need filling. Smokey let out a contented sigh, his paws twitching as if chasing something in his dreams. The air was warm but carried the promise of cooler night breezes, and the faint scent of Evelyn's gardenias wafted from the flowerbeds lining the porch.

"You know," Evelyn said softly, her gaze fixed on the horizon, "there was a time I never thought I'd have this. A home, this kind of peace. You."

Cass glanced at her, surprised by the vulnerability in her voice. Evelyn wasn't one to dwell on the past or wear her emotions on her sleeve. It made these moments all the more precious.

"Yeah," Cass said, her voice low. "Me too. Thought I'd spend my whole life chasing fires and barking orders. Didn't think I'd have time for anything else."

"And now?" Evelyn asked, turning to look at her.

Cass reached for her hand, their fingers intertwining. "Now I've got everything I need right here."

Evelyn's lips curved into a soft smile, and for a moment, neither of them said anything. The sun sank lower, its light fading into a dusky purple. The first stars began to appear, tiny pinpricks of light against the darkening sky.

"You're getting sappy on me, Harris," Evelyn said after a beat, her tone light but her expression warm.

Cass chuckled, squeezing her hand. "Don't get used to it."

They lapsed into silence again, but this time Evelyn leaned over, resting her head on Cass's shoulder. Cass shifted slightly, wrapping an arm around her. It was an instinctive gesture, one born of years spent learning the rhythm of each other's presence.

"You know," Evelyn murmured, her voice muffled against Cass's shoulder, "I still think about that first argument we had. In your office, about...what was it? Fire truck maintenance budgets?"

Cass laughed softly. "You mean the one where you were wrong?"

Evelyn lifted her head just enough to glare at her. "I wasn't wrong. You were being stubborn."

"And you were being impossible," Cass countered, her grin widening.

"Fair," Evelyn conceded with a mock sigh, settling back against her shoulder. "And yet, here we are."

"Here we are," Cass echoed, her voice tinged with affection.

Smokey stirred at their feet, letting out a small huff before curling into a tighter ball. Cass absently reached down to pat his side, her gaze drifting upward to the sky. The stars were coming out in earnest now, the constellations twinkling like old friends.

"You ever think about what's next?" Evelyn asked quietly.

Cass tilted her head, considering. "Not really. I figure we'll just keep doing what we're doing. You with your pamphlets, me with my rookies. Maybe take a vacation someday, if you can pry yourself away from your meetings."

Evelyn hummed thoughtfully. "A vacation sounds nice. Somewhere warm, maybe. With no cell service."

"No cell service?" Cass teased. "You'd last, what, a day?"

"I'd last two," Evelyn said with mock indignation. "Maybe three."

Cass laughed, the sound low and genuine. She tightened her arm around Evelyn, pressing a kiss to her temple. "Whatever's next, we'll figure it out."

They sat there as the evening deepened, the stars shining brighter with every passing moment. The porch, their home, this quiet life they had built together—it wasn't flashy or dramatic, but it was theirs. And that was enough.

As the last traces of daylight disappeared, Evelyn sighed contentedly. "I'm glad it's you, Cass. It's always been you."

Cass didn't reply right away, letting the words settle in her chest like a warm glow. Finally, she said, "And I'm glad it's you."

They stayed that way, wrapped up in each other, until the night was full and still. And as Cass looked out at the vast sky, she felt the kind of peace she'd once thought was impossible—a life of love, balance, and quiet joy, shared with the person who had become her everything.

FREE BOOK

I really hope you enjoyed this story. I loved writing it.

I'd love for you to get my FREE book- Her Boss- by joining my mailing list. On my mailing list you can be the first to find out about free or discounted books or new releases and get short sexy stories for free! Just click on the following link or type into your web browser: https://BookHip.com/MNVVPBP

Meg has had a huge crush on her hot older boss for some time now. Could it be possible that her crush is reciprocated? https://BookHip.com/MNVVPBP

FREE BOOK

If you like Phoenix Ridge Fire, I think you will love my Hearts Medical Series. Super hot Sapphic Surgeons... More fierce lesbian firefighters.. don't miss it! Start with Book 1: Rules of the Heart

Can she break her own rules and take a chance on love?
mybook.to/Hearts1

Printed in Great Britain
by Amazon